BREAKING THE CODE

by Hugh Whitemore

Based on the book
Alan Turing: The Enigma
by Andrew Hodges

A SAMUEL FRENCH ACTING EDITION

SAMUEL FRENCH

FOUNDED 1830

New York Hollywood London Toronto
SAMUELFRENCH.COM

IMPORTANT BILLING AND CREDIT REQUIREMENTS

The London premiere of BREAKING THE CODE was first presented by Michael Redington in association with Duncan C. Weldon and Jerome Minskoff at the Yvonne Arnaud Theatre, Guilford on September 15th, 1986, and subsequently at the Theatre Royal, Haymarket, London on October 21, 1986 with the following cast:

Alan Turing.......................... Derek Jacobi
Mick Ross .... Dave Hill
Christopher Morcom .... Richard Stirling
Sara Turing.......................... Isobel Dean
Ron Miller .... Paul Slack
John Smith .... Michael Malnick
Dillwyn Knox .... Michael Gough
Pat Green .... Joanna David
Nikos............................... Dean Winters

Director: Clifford Williams
Set and costumes: Liz da Costa
Lighting Designer: Mick Hughes

The New York Premiere of BREAKING THE CODE was produced by Jerome Minskoff, Duncan C. Weldon, James M. Nederlander, The Kennedy Center/A.N.T.A. by arrangement with Triumph Theatre Productions, Ltd. and Michael Redington. BREAKING THE CODE opened on Broadway at the Neil Simon Theatre on November 15, 1987 with the following cast:

Alan Turing.......................... Derek Jacobi
Mick Ross .... Colm Meaney
Christopher Morcom .... Robert Sean Leonard
Sara Turing .... Rachel Gurney
Ron Miller .... Michael Dolan
John Smith......................... Richard Clarke
Dillwyn Knox .... Michael Gough
Pat Green.......................... Jenny Agutter
Nikos .... Andreas Manolikakis

Director: Clifford Williams
Set and costumes: Liz da Costa
Lighting Designer: Natasha Katz

CHARACTERS
(in order of appearance)

MICK ROSS

ALAN TURING

CHRISTOPHER MORCOM

SARA TURING

RON MILLER

JOHN SMITH

DILLWYN KNOX

PAT GREEN

NIKOS

BREAKING THE CODE

ACT I
Scene 1

AT RISE: Winter afternoon. ALAN TURING Enters with MICK ROSS.

TURING is about 40. untidily dressed, unkempt appearance; an occasional stammer. ROSS is carrying a file; he is a Detective Sergeant.

Ross. Sorry to keep you waiting, sir. Sit down. *(TURING sits; ROSS sits facing him.)* Make yourself comfortable. *(Opens the file.)* Well now, let's get the basic facts sorted out. We're talking about a burglary that occurred on January the 23rd and you are Mr. Spurling.

TURING. No—Turing.

Ross. I beg your pardon?

TURING. My name is Turing, *not* Spurling.

Ross. Sorry, sir, beg your pardon. Bloody illiterate, some of our young constables. *(Displays a sheet of paper.)* Just look at this atrocious writing. It could be Spurling, Spilling, Tilling.

TURING. Well, it's Turing. *(spelling)* T-U-R-I-N-G.

Ross. *(writing)* Alan Mathison Turing. Is that right?

TURING. Yes.

ROSS. Right. Mick Ross. Detective Sergeant.

TURING. How do you do.

ROSS. How do you do, sir. *(Looks at the file of papers.)* You live at Hollymeade, Adlington Road, Wilmslow?

TURING. Yes.

ROSS. And you work at Manchester University?

TURING. Yes.

ROSS. So it's Professor Turing?

TURING. Mr. Turing is perfectly adequate.

ROSS. Right. *(Glances at TURING.)* Not a native north-countryman?

TURING. No.

ROSS. No, I thought not. How long have you been here?

TURING. Four years; since 1948.

ROSS. *(As he writes.)* It's an unusual name. Turing. Don't think I've come across it before.

TURING. Scottish.

ROSS. Ah. Whereabouts?

TURING. I'm sorry...?

ROSS. Whereabouts in Scotland do you come from?

TURING. No, I, um — the Turings are of Scottish descent—

ROSS. I see.

TURING. —they came to England some time ago.

ROSS. Before you were born?

TURING. In the 17th century, I think.

ROSS. Ah — right. *(A grin; then looks at the file.)* Now, sir, this burglary: can you tell me exactly what happened?

TURING. Well, as I explained to the police constable, I

got back home on Wednesday evening and found that the house had been broken into. *(pause)*

Ross. Yes...?

Turing. I telephoned the police and then I made a list of what was missing — of what seemed to be missing.

Ross. *(Showing a sheet of paper to TURING.)* Is this your list?

Turing. *(Looks at sheet.)* Yes.

Ross. A shirt, five fish knives, a pair of tweed trousers, three pairs of shoes, a compass, an electric shaver, and a half-empty bottle of sherry. Not much of a haul.

Turing. No, I don't, uh...

Ross. Yes, sir?

Turing. I live very simply. Possessions, *per se,* mean very little to me.

Ross. Possessions what, sir?

Turing. What?

Ross. I didn't hear what you said.

Turing. Possessions *per se:* for their own sake.

Ross. Ah yes. *(Refers to the report.)* Now you said — you said to the constable — you told him that you had some idea who might've committed the crime. Is that so?

Turing. Well, yes. *(Brief pause; ROSS waits.)* I think his name is George.

Ross. George...?

Turing. Yes.

Ross. George what?

Turing. I don't know.

Ross. Who is this man? Do you know him?

Turing. No.

Ross. Can you describe him?

TURING. No, I've never seen him.

ROSS. But you know his name?

TURING. Well yes, somebody told me.

ROSS. Told you what, sir?

TURING. That this man George might be a burglar.

ROSS. Who told you?

TURING. Well, um — a young man came to the door. He was selling something. Brushes or something. He told me to be careful because, uh ... he'd heard somebody talking about a burglary. They were planning a burglary, you see. He overheard them.

ROSS. *(eyebrows raised)* He heard this man George making some sort of plan to burgle your house?

TURING. Not my house specifically, no. A house in my neighbourhood. Or so I gather. That's what I was told. This young man — the brush salesman — he said he knew the person who was talking. George. He recognized him, do you see? And, um ... well, that's all, really.

ROSS. Where did this conversation take place?

TURING. What conversation?

ROSS. The conversation this young man overheard.

TURING. In a pub, I think.

ROSS. In a pub?

TURING. I think so, yes.

ROSS. *(frowns)* I'm puzzled, Mr. Turing. How did the subject come up? Why did this brush salesman decide to tell you about a conversation he'd overheard in a pub?

TURING. Well, I suppose ... to warn me, I suppose.

ROSS. It's very curious, don't you think? It's an odd

thing to have happened.

TURING. Is it?

Ross. I'd have thought so. Why didn't you inform the police at the time?

TURING. It never occurred to me to do so. I mean, it was only a casual remark. He just said be careful, keep your eyes open. I didn't pay much attention, really.

Ross. Mmm. *(A moment of reflection.)* When did he come to your house?

TURING. Three or four weeks ago.

Ross. Who did he work for, do you remember?

TURING. I've no idea.

Ross. What sort of brushes was he selling?

TURING. It may not have been brushes. I forget.

Ross. It'd be useful if you could remember.

TURING. Yes, I'll try.

Ross. Please do.

(The telephone rings.)

Ross. Excuse me, sir. *(Goes to phone, lifts the receiver.)* Hello, Ross ... Yes? ... When? ... Right. *(Replaces the receiver; picks up the file.)* Sorry, sir — bit of a problem. *(Rises to his feet.)* We'll be in touch, okay? One of the lads will show you out. *(ROSS Exits.)*

Scene 2

SCENE: Lighting change: Summer afternoon.

AT RISE: TURING is on stage. CHRISTOPHER MORCOM enters, wearing a school uniform; he is about 17.

CHRIS. He should never have lied; that was the real mistake. I have some very definite ideas of right and wrong, and it's always wrong to lie.

TURING. Perhaps he was afraid.

CHRIS. *(Takes off coat.)* Of course he was afraid. He's cheated during the Latin exam; he knew he'd be found out, he knew he'd be punished. But lying made everything a hundred times worse.

SARA. *(offstage)* Alan! Alan!

TURING. Oh, Lord — that's my mother.

(SARA Enters; she wears clothes appropriate for the late 1920's.)

SARA. Ah, here you are. Do forgive me. I thought I heard the doorbell, but I wasn't sure, I was out in the garden, you see. Do forgive me. *(A brief, rather awkward silence.)* Alan, dear, won't you introduce your friend?

TURING. *(gracelessly)* Oh, sorry — this is Christopher Morcom.

SARA. *(extends hand)* How do you do, Christopher.

12

CHRIS. *(shake hands)* How do you do, Mrs. Turing.

SARA. I'm delighted to meet you at long last. Alan has talked so much about you, and I kept saying to him, "Do invite Christopher down for a weekend" — never expecting for a moment that he would. No matter what we say, he always endeavours to keep his school friends to himself. I think perhaps he's ashamed of us. *(TURING squirms; CHRIS responds with a shy smile.)* Did you have a comfortable journey

CHRIS. Yes, thank you. The train was almost empty.

SARA. Oh, good. *(Smiles at him.)* Do sit down, won't you? Sit over here, by me.

CHRIS. Thank you. *(SARA and CHRIS sit by the table.)*

SARA. Alan tells me that your family has a place in town.

CHRIS. Well, it's only very small; near Victoria Station, actually. My mother uses it as a studio.

SARA. A studio?

CHRIS. For her sculpture. She makes sculptures and so on.

SARA. How exciting.

CHRIS. Well, not really.

SARA. Isn't it? I would've thought it would be rather exciting to have a mother who is an artist.

CHRIS. It's only a hobby, really. She spends most of her time looking after the goats.

SARA. What goats?

CHRIS. We have a goat farm at home.

SARA. Near Victoria Station?

CHRIS. No, in the country. Our real home is in Worcestershire.

SARA. I love Worcestershire: the garden of England.

TURING. That's Kent, Mother.

SARA. *(ignoring this)* I often wish we'd been able to spend more time in England, but of course that wasn't possible. Has Alan told you about our travels?

CHRIS. No.

SARA. Ah, well — my husband was in the Indian Civil Service. He's retired now. Ill health. But for years we roamed around India: Bezwada, Madras, Kurnool, Chatrapur. Alan was very nearly born in Chatrapur.

TURING. How can you be nearly born somewhere? It doesn't make sense.

SARA. *(irritated)* Oh, Alan — please.

TURING. Look at it logically.

SARA. I do wish you wouldn't say things like that.

TURING. Like what?

SARA. You know how much it annoys me. *(to CHRIS:)* Alan has such an unruly streak in his nature. I'm sure you're much more level-headed.

CHRIS. Well, I...

SARA. *(not waiting)* Anyway, I'm glad that you've become such firm friends. Without a steadying influence it's all too easy for a clever boy to grow into a mere intellectual crank.

TURING. *(tartly)* Thank you, Mother.

SARA. I don't mean that unkindly; it's a very real danger. *(to CHRIS:)* How long have you been at Sherborne?

CHRIS. A year longer than Turing. *(correcting himself)* Alan.

SARA. Are you enjoying it?

CHRIS. Very much.

SARA. Choosing the right school is so tremendously important, don't you think? — and I'm very impressed with Sherborne.

TURING. It's not that wonderful.

SARA. Of course it is. *(glancing sharply)* What's wrong with it?

TURING. Well, for one thing, they don't treat mathematics as a serious subject.

SARA. I can't believe that.

TURING. It's true. Do you know what our form-master said the other day? "This room stinks of mathematics," he said, looking straight at me, "go out and get a disinfectant spray." *(CHRIS laughs.)*

SARA. He was joking.

TURING. He hates anything to do with mathematics or science. He once said — and he meant it — he said the Germans lost The Great War because they thought that science was more important than religion.

SARA. The teaching of mathematics is not the only way to judge the quality of a school.

TURING. It is as far as I'm concerned.

SARA. Oh, Alan. *(To CHRIS.)* I gather you share this enthusiasm for sums and science?

CHRIS. Oh yes, very much so. And it's wonderful having someone like Alan to work with. Has he told you about our experiments?

SARA. A little. Wasn't there something to do with iodine?

TURING. Iodates, Mother.

CHRIS. We were trying to examine the time delay in

the recombination of ions.

SARA. Yes, it was all far beyond my grasp, I'm afraid. Fascinating, but beyond my grasp. It was the same with that theory Alan was telling me about — *(to TURING:)* — what was it? — you know, the man with the Jewish name.

TURING. Einstein.

SARA. Einstein, yes: I didn't understand a word of it — not one word. I only wish I did. Does your family understand these things?

CHRIS. Well, yes — up to a point.

TURING. Morcom's brother is a scientist. They've got their own laboratory at home.

SARA. Really?

TURING. And he's got his own telescope.

SARA. Really? — how splendid.

CHRIS. It's tremendous, Mrs. Turing — absolutely terrific. The other night — *(to TURING:)* — did I tell you? — the other night I actually saw one of Jupiter's satellites coming out from eclipse. It was amazing. It was a wonderfully clear night. Absolutely cloudless. I felt I was wandering through the universe. Jupiter, Sirius, Betelgeuse, the Andromeda nebula. It was quite overwhelming. The hugeness of creation.

TURING. Gosh, how terrific.

SARA. Yes, it all sounds very thrilling, I must say. But I do hope you don't frighten your family the way Alan does. *(TURING sighs with irritation.)*

CHRIS. Frighten them how?

SARA. He got up at three o'clock in the morning last Thursday — I can't imagine why — I woke up and heard footsteps on the stairs. I was convinced that we had burglars in the house, and my husband was on the point of telephoning to the police when we realized that it was only Alan.

TURING. I was mapping the constellations of fixed stars.

SARA. I sometimes wish he was interested in stamp collecting or model trains, like his brother. *(TURING snorts with displeasure; SARA rises to her feet; CHRIS follows suit.)* Let's have some tea, shall we? *(to TURING:)* Do wash your hands, they're covered in ink. *(to CHRIS:)* Did Alan tell you about my grandfather's cousin? He was a scientist. He invented the electron.

TURING. He didn't invent it, Mother; electrons exist, you can't invent them.

SARA. Well, he found them, or discovered them, or something like that. He was a Fellow of the Royal Society. Very distinguished. *(to TURING as she Exits:)* Do wash your hands. *(TURING grimaces to CHRIS.)*

TURING. Sorry, Morcom — one can't choose one's own mother.

CHRIS. *(a grin)* She's all right. *(TURING takes a step towards CHRIS.)*

TURING. Do you know what I wish?

CHRIS. What?

TURING. I wish this was my house. My own house. Then we could live here, you and I. We could have our own rooms, our own laboratories. We could work together. Share everything. What a wonderful life that would be.

CHRIS. *(Looks at TURING.)* Yes. Yes, it would.

SARA. *(offstage)* Come along, Christopher!

CHRIS. I'd better go. *(CHRIS turns to leave.)*

TURING. Chris. *(CHRIS pauses.)* Thank you for coming to see me. *(CHRIS smiles.)*

CHRIS. Don't forget to wash your hands. *(CHRIS exits.)*

Scene 3

SCENE: LIGHTING change: Winter evening.

AT RISE: TURING sits at a table.

> *RON MILLER Enters; he is about 20, north-country, working-class; he is holding a mug of beer. He looks at TURING, hesitates for a moment, then strolls to the table.*

RON. Anyone sitting here?

TURING. No. *(RON sits, drinks some beer; looks around.)*

RON. Quiet tonight.

TURING. Yes. Very.

RON. All the pubs are the same. I've just been down The King's Head. Same as this place. Nobody around.

TURING. Perhaps it's the weather.

RON. Yeah. Bloody cold.

TURING. Real Christmas weather.

RON. Bloody Christmas. *(drinks)* Christmas in Manchester: the bleedin' bitter end. *(TURING smiles.)*

TURING. I saw you in here last week.

RON. Yeah, could be. Yeah — I often come in here. God knows why. Quiet as the bloody grave. *(drinks)* I should've stayed at The King's Head. They've got a jukebox down there. That livens it up a bit. All the latest hits, Johnnie Ray, Guy Mitchell, Frankie Laine. *(pause)* Still, it's handy here.

TURING. Handy for work?

RON. No, no — just — you know — handy.

TURING. Where do you work?

RON. I don't. Not at the moment. I had a job making spectacle frames. Then the bloody government starts making cuts. No more free teeth and glasses on the National Health. Bang goes the job. Bye-bye, they said — piss off.

TURING. That's bad luck.

RON. You're telling me. So I'm stuck at home. Not much fun in that. *(drinks)* What about you?

TURING. I've got my own place.

RON. I meant your job.

TURING. I'm at the university.

RON. Bit old for that, aren't you?

TURING. I'm on the staff.

RON. A teacher?

TURING. Not exactly. I do, um ... well, research work.

RON. What sort?

TURING. Scientific. Mathematics. Actually, we're trying to build a special sort of machine. What people call the Electronic Brain.

RON. *(Stares at TURING.)* Bloody hell, that sounds a bit like...

Turing. Like what?

Ron. Sounds like that film.

Turing. What film?

Ron. Michael Rennie. I saw it when I was down in London. Michael Rennie and some sort of robot. *(remembering)* The Day the Earth Stood Still. Did you see it?

Turing. No.

Ron. Bloody good. *(drinks)* So what's it do, this thing you're making?

Turing. You give it problems — mathematical problems — and it solves them very quickly.

Ron. How quickly?

Turing. Very, very quickly. Far more quickly than a man could.

Ron. Like an adding machine?

Turing. No, it's more than that. We're trying to make a machine that can learn things and eventually think for itself.

Ron. Think for itself...?

Turing. Why not?

Ron. Bloody hell.

Turing. It's not a robot — and it's not really a brain. Not like the human brain, anyway. It's what we call a digital computer. *(RON is impressed.)*

Ron. You thought this up, did you?

Turing. Sort of.

Ron. Must be interesting, a job like that.

Turing. It is.

Ron. Good money, too, I bet.

Turing. Not bad.

Ron. *(RON drinks.)* I once fancied being a chemist.

Must've been about fourteen. Don't know why. Just fancied the idea of it somehow.

TURING. Did you do anything about it?

RON. Bought myself a chemistry set. Blew the bloody windows out. That was the end of that. *(TURING smiles. RON drinks.)*

TURING. Look, um... would you like something to eat? There's a cafe across the road.

RON. No, I can't really, not now, I—

TURING. *(quickly, not wishing to be snubbed)* Right. *(Brief pause. RON glances at TURING.)*

RON. How about some other time?

TURING. Yes, all right. When?

RON. Don't mind.

TURING. This weekend?

RON. If you like.

TURING. What about Friday evening?

RON. Okay.

TURING. Come to my house.

RON. *(a brief hesitation)* Okay. *(TURING takes a scrap of paper from his pocket and writes his address.)*

TURING. This is the address. Come to my house. *(He gives the note to RON.)* Do you know where it is?

RON. I can find it.

TURING. Come about seven. I'll cook you a meal.

RON. Good cook, are you?

TURING. Not bad. *(smiles)* What's your name?

RON. Ron.

TURING. Alan. *(Extends hand, shakes. RON finishes his beer; he stands up.)*

RON. Okay, Alan — I'll see you Friday.

TURING. About seven.
RON. About seven.
TURING. Don't change your mind.
RON. *(a grin)* I'll be there. *(RON Exits.)*

Scene 4

SCENE: LIGHTING change: Winter morning.

AT RISE: ROSS Enters.

ROSS. We're having a bit of a problem with regard to this brush salesman you were telling us about.
TURING. Oh?
ROSS. We spoke to some of your neighbors. No one seems to have seen him but you. I don't understand it.
TURING. Perhaps they were out when he called.
ROSS. All of them?
TURING. It's possible.
ROSS. And we checked with the local domestic appliance firms. None of them have had a salesman working in your area.
TURING. Well, as I said, I might've been mistaken.
ROSS. What about?
TURING. What he was doing, what he was selling.
ROSS. I can't believe you'd make a mistake like that, sir. You must've been talking to him for several minutes.

At least. Weren't you?

TURING. As I recall, I was rather preoccupied. I was working, you see, and, uh ... well, to be honest, I don't remember much about him.

ROSS. What did he look like? You must remember what he looked like.

TURING. Not really. Youngish. Ordinary. I really didn't take much notice of him.

ROSS. You didn't, did you, sir?

TURING. Well, no.

ROSS. Why not?

TURING. He was only a travelling salesman, after all.

ROSS. Even so ... all that talk about burglars and suspicious characters — I'd have made sure I knew what he looked like.

TURING. Perhaps that's because you're a policeman.

ROSS. Could be.

TURING. Anyway, why is he so important? Surely it's the burglar you should be looking for.

ROSS. Supposing he wasn't a brush salesman. Supposing he was somehow involved in the burglary.

TURING. *(a hint of alarm)* What makes you think that?

ROSS. He might even be the burglar. It's an old trick: he knocks on the door, if no one answers, in he goes. The brush salesman story is just camouflage.

TURING. That doesn't make sense.

ROSS. Why not?

TURING. If he was involved in the burglary, why should he pretend to warn me?

ROSS. *(shrugs)* People do funny things.

TURING. Oh look, this is ridiculous. I feel I'm making a fuss about nothing. I didn't lose very much, well, hardly anything. I can't think why I bothered to report it.

Ross. I'm glad you did, sir. All crimes should be reported: big and small.

TURING. It all seems to trivial.

Ross. Trivial...?

TURING. Don't you think?

Ross. Well, that's our problem now, so don't you worry about it. Okay?

TURING. *(a reluctant nod)* If you say so.

Ross. Good. *(Goes to the door.)* If you remember anything — no matter how trivial it may seem — I'd be grateful if you'd let me know.

TURING. All right. *(ROSS opens the door for TURING.)*

Ross. You won't be leaving Manchester, will you, sir?

TURING. *(a frown)* How do you mean?

Ross. Just in case I need to talk to you.

TURING. Oh no — no, no ... well, I'll be in London next week, just for a couple of days.

Ross. When?

TURING. Tuesday and Wednesday. I'm doing a broadcast.

Ross. Oh really?

TURING. A talk — you know — a discussion.

Ross. What about?

TURING. Er — machines. Can machines think? Is it possible to build a machine that thinks for itself?

Ross. Sounds interesting. When's it on?

TURING. Tuesday evening, eight o'clock.

Ross. Well, I'll listen. Make a point of it. *(He shakes TURING by the hand.)* Thanks very much, Mr. Turing. I'll give you a ring if anything turns up.

Turing. Thank you. *(TURING Exits U.R.)*

(JOHN SMITH Enters: middle-aged, wearing a dark city suit; his voice is authoritative: upper-class.)

Smith. What do you think?

Ross. A bit of a joke, him doing a broadcast with a stammer like that.

Smith. About the burglary.

Ross. I'm not sure, sir. It doesn't add up, somehow. He's not telling us everything.

Smith. Do you think he's lying?

Ross. I think he might be. *(SMITH considers this for a moment; then he goes to the door; ROSS follows.)*

Smith. Let me know what happens. Your superintendent knows where to find me.

Ross. Yes, sir.

Smith. Handle it carefully, Ross; carefully and discreetly. There are certain anxieties. The Foreign Office wants to avoid any possible embarrassment.

Ross. *(surprised)* I didn't know he was mixed up with the Foreign Office.

Smith. He got to be their chap during the war. Quite a big fish, our Mr. Turing. Winston thought the world of him.

(SMITH and ROSS Exit.)

Scene 5

SCENE: LIGHTING change: Autumn afternoon.

AT RISE: TURING Enters with DILLWYN KNOX. KNOX is about 60; Eton and King's; walks with a slight limp; he is carrying a bulky file.

KNOX. So you found us all right?

TURING. Yes, thank you, no problems.

KNOX. Silly question, really. I mean, here you are. Of course you found us. *(Puts the file on a table.)* Punctual to the minute. Bravo. That's quite an achievement these days. If only Churchill could take a leaf out of Mussolini's book and make the trains run on time. Which one did you catch?

TURING. I got here this morning, actually.

KNOX. This morning?

TURING. I didn't want to be late.

KNOX. You've been here all day?

TURING. Yes.

KNOX. Oh dear, poor you. Bletchley doesn't have much to offer — as you must have discovered.

TURING. I went to the cinema.

KNOX. Well, exactly. Nothing else to do here. What did you see?

TURING. A cartoon film: *Snow White and the Seven Dwarfs.*

KNOX. I think I saw it; I took one of my nieces. I invariably fall asleep at the cinema. Isn't there a wicked witch?

TURING. Yes, she gives Snow White a poisoned apple.

KNOX. Don't tell me it's got a sad ending.

TURING. No, she wakes up in the arms of a handsome prince. It's really quite touching.

KNOX. Really?

TURING. Well, in a sentimental sort of way.

KNOX. Obviously I wasn't paying enough attention. I must make a point of seeing it again sometime. *(He sits; TURING sits.)* You must be wondering what this is all about.

TURING. I know your reputation as a code-breaker, Mr. Knox, so I assumed it was something to do with the deciphering work you're doing here.

KNOX. Ah. You've heard about that.

TURING. Nothing much, just talk.

KNOX. What sort of talk?

TURING. Amongst my colleagues at Cambridge. *(KNOX is clearly disconcerted.)*

KNOX. It's supposed to be tremendously secret, this place — I mean quite tremendously secret. Hence all the barbed wire and soldiers and passwords and so on.

TURING. Yes, I realize that.

KNOX. How did you get in, by the way? Did they tell you the password?

TURING. I showed them your letter.

KNOX. Oh good, well done. I always make a frightful balls-up of this password nonsense. It must be something to do with my age.

TURING. In what respect?

KNOX. Failing memory. We all live far too long, that's the trouble: faculties fade, the body disintegrates, the mind crumbles. My solicitor says that dentists are to blame. He opines that nature intended us to die as soon as our teeth drop out; but thanks to the advances in dentistry, we struggle on into an infirm and wretched old age. *(brief pause)* Yes...?

TURING. I didn't speak.

KNOX. What was I saying?

TURING. Passwords.

KNOX. Ah yes. We're supposed to call this place Station X, but of course, everyone knows it's the Government Code and Cipher School: the G.C.C.S. — waggishly referred to as the Golf Club and Chess Society. *(He laughs; TURING smiles; KNOX opens the file.)* You'll have to bear with me, Turing; I'm not an administrator, neither am I a mathematician — but since it seems highly likely that we shall be working together, the powers-that-be think we should have some sort of exploratory conversation. Is that all right with you?

TURING. Of course.

KNOX. Good. *(Indicates a file.)* This is your file. I shall consult it from time to time. There's no need to be alarmed.

TURING. I'm not.

KNOX. Good. *(Looks at the file.)* So you went to Sherborne, Cambridge, *(some surprise)* — and then America: 1936 to 1938; two years in America. How was that? Did you enjoy Princeton?

TURING. Well, yes, it was ... yes.

KNOX. Enjoy is scarcely the right word, perhaps.

TURING. No, no, as a matter of fact, it was very enjoyable — some of it, anyway. Peculiar, too, until I got used to it.

KNOX. In what way peculiar?

TURING. Oh, many ways: peculiar clothes, peculiar food, peculiar habits of speech. Whenever you thank them for anything, Americans always say, "you're welcome." I found this rather charming at first — thinking they meant that I was indeed welcome. But in fact it's just a conversational tic; it comes back like a ball thrown against a wall: extremely irritating.

KNOX. Aha.

TURING. They say that a lot too.

KNOX. Say what?

TURING. Aha. When they can't think of a suitable reply, but think silence would be rude, they tend to say, "Aha."

KNOX. *(TURING'S sharpness makes him a little uneasy.)* I see. Fascinating. What exactly did you do there?

TURING. Um ... well, I'd just published a paper, "On Computable Numbers," and I was able to develop some of those ideas and, uh ... various other things, various other research projects.

KNOX. All concerned with mathematics and logic?

TURING. Yes.

KNOX. Yes. *(turning a page)* And your interest in codes and ciphers: how did that begin?

TURING. I've always been interested, I think, ever since I was a boy. I got a prize at school: a book called

Mathematical Recreations and Essays. There was a chapter on cryptography. I found it fascinating and I suppose it focused my interest in ciphers. And then, much more recently — when I got back from America — I realized that my ideas in mathematics and logic might be applied to ciphers. That, of course, created something of a dilemma.

KNOX. Why?

TURING. I realized that such knowledge would acquire military value if war were declared. I was concerned about the moral implications of putting my, uh — intellectual armory — at the disposal of a government at war.

KNOX. Have you managed to resolve this dilemma?

TURING. Well, I'm here. Doesn't that answer your question?

KNOX. Not necessarily. I gather you were a supporter of the anti-war movement at Cambridge?

TURING. In 1933, yes.

KNOX. Would you describe yourself as a pacifist?

TURING. No, I wouldn't.

KNOX. You've changed your mind?

TURING. No, I've always thought that some wars could be justified.

KNOX. Justified how?

TURING. As a lesser evil in the last resort. Hitler has brought us to that last resort.

KNOX. So you would regard this war as a necessary evil?

TURING. First and foremost, I regard this war as a most unfortunate interruption to my work. But also — yes, you're right — I do think of it as a necessary evil.

KNOX. What about loyalty to your country — a sense of duty: do these considerations carry any weight with you?

TURING. *(bristling)* As it happens, England and things English mean a very great deal to me — but whenever I hear people appealing to my sense of patriotism, I feel that I'm being made to do something I don't want to do. *(firmly)* I have come here because I have decided for myself what I should do in the current circumstances. The work sounds intriguing. I think I'd be more useful here than on a battlefield.

KNOX. Do not imagine that the nature of the work we do will protect you from the moral responsibility for killing and destruction. Sometimes very hard decisions have to be made. How do you feel about that?

TURING. I have always been willing — indeed eager — to accept moral responsibility for what I do.

KNOX. Good. *(a small smile)* Good! *(consulting the file; turning a page)* I've been furnished with some details of your work, Mr. Turing, most of which I have to tell you I find almost totally incomprehensible.

TURING. That's hardly surprising.

KNOX. I knew quite a bit about mathematics when I was young, but this is — well baffling. *(Studies file.)* For example ... this thing here: "On Computable Numbers with an Application to the *Ent-scheid-ungs-prob-lem.*" *(He raises his head and looks at TURING.)* Perhaps you could tell me about it.

TURING. Tell you what?

KNOX. Well, anything — a few words of explanation — in general terms.

TURING. *(TURING is amused.)* A few words of explanation?

KNOX. Yes.

TURING. In general terms?

KNOX. If possible.

TURING. It's about right and wrong. In general terms. It's a technical paper in mathematical logic, but it's also about the difficulty of telling right from wrong. *(brief pause)* People think — most people think — that in mathematics we always know what is right and what is wrong. Not so. Not any more. It's a problem that's occupied mathematicians for forty or fifty years. How can you tell right from wrong? Bertrand Russell wrote an immense book about it: *Principia Mathematica.* His idea was to break down all mathematical concepts and arguments into little bits and then show that they could be derived from pure logic; but it didn't quite work, all he was able to do was to show that it's terribly difficult to do anything of the kind. But it was an important book. Important and influential. It influenced both David Hilbert and Kurt Gödel. *(a brief digression)*

It's rather like what physicists call splitting the atom. As analyzing the physical atom has led to the discovery of a new kind of physics, so the attempt to analyze these mathematical atoms has led to a new kind of mathematics. *(resuming the main thread of his explanation)*

Hilbert took the whole thing a stage further. I don't suppose his name means much to you — if anything — well, there we are, that's the way of the world: people never seem to hear of the really great mathematicians. Hilbert looked at the problem from a completely different angle and he said, if we are going to have any fundamental system for mathematics — like the one Russell was trying to work out — it must satisfy three basic requirements: consistency, completeness and decidability. Consistency means that you won't ever get a contradiction in your own system; in other words, you'll never be able to follow the rules of your system and end up by showing that two and two make five. Completeness means that if any statement is true, there must be some way of proving it by using the rules of your system. And decidability means that there must exist some method, some definite procedure or test, which can be applied to any given mathematical assertion and which will decide whether or not that assertion is provable. Hilbert thought this was a very reasonable set of requirements to impose; but within a few years, Kurt Gödel showed that no system for mathematics could be both consistent and complete. He did this by constructing a mathematical assertion that said — in effect: "This assertion cannot be proved." A classic paradox. "This assertion cannot be proved." Well, either it can or it can't. If it can be proved, we have a contradiction, and the system is inconsistent. If it cannot be proved, then the assertion is true — but it can't be proved; which means that the system is complete. Thus mathematics is either inconsistent or it's incomplete. It's a beautiful theorem, quite beautiful. I think Gödel's theorem is the most beautiful thing I know. But the question of decidability was still unresolved. As I said, Hilbert thought there should be a single clearly defined method for deciding whether or not mathematical assertions were provable. The decision problem, he called it. The *Entscheidungsproblem.* In my paper "On

Computable Numbers," I wanted to show that there can be no one method that will work for all questions. Solving mathematical problems requires an infinite supply of new ideas. It was, of course, a monumental task to prove such a thing. One needed to examine the probability of all mathematical assertions past, present and future. How on earth could this be done? Eventually one word gave me the clue. People had been talking about the possibility of a mechanical process, a process that could be applied mechanically to solving mathematical problems without requiring any human intervention or ingenuity. Machine! — that was the crucial word. I conceived the idea of a machine, a Turing machine, that would be able to scan mathematical symbols — to read them, if you like — to read a mathematical assertion and to arrive at the verdict as to whether or not that assertion were provable. With this concept I was able to prove that Hilbert was wrong. My idea worked.

KNOX. You actually built this machine?

TURING. No, no — it was a machine of the imagination, like one of Einstein's thought experiments. Building it wasn't important; it's a perfectly clear idea, after all.

KNOX. Yes, I see; well, I don't, but I see something — I think. *(He looks at TURING.)* Forgive me for asking a crass and naive question — but what is the point of devising a machine that cannot be built in order to prove that there are certain mathematical statements that cannot be proved? Is there any practical value in all this?

TURING. The possibilities are boundless. In my paper, "On Computable Numbers," I explain how a special kind of Turing machine — I call it the Universal Machine — could carry out any process that can be described in symbols. In fact, I believe it could carry out any mental process whatsoever.

KNOX. *(a small smile)* The originality of your thinking is clearly remarkable; and I'm sure that you'll prove to be an invaluable member of our team, group, call it what you will. *(Closes the file.)* We'd like you to start work immediately. Is that all right?

TURING. Of course.

KNOX. Are there any questions you want to ask me?

TURING. Not really; my only anxiety is about my fitting into a place like this. I've never been very good at organizing things — least of all myself — and I'm not sure how well I'll function in a government department.

KNOX. You mustn't worry about that. There's a healthy disregard of organizational formality at G.C.C.S. — if there weren't, I wouldn't be here. As far as I'm concerned, rules are only important in cricket, poetry and scholarly editing of ancient texts. *(Smiles; goes to the door.)* I'm going to ask Miss Green to join us. *(Opens the door.)* Will you ask Pat to come in, please? *(Returns to TURING.)* Patricia Green is one of our most able cryptanalysts. Quite as good as any chap.

TURING. What sort of work shall I be doing?

KNOX. You'll be concentrating on something called the Enigma code. It's been devised and developed by the Germans — and it's an absolute pig.

(PAT appears at the door.)

KNOX. Ah — Pat. Do come in. *(She Enters and closes the door.)* Come and meet Alan Turing.

PAT. How do you do.

TURING. How do you do. *(They shake hands.)*

PAT. Actually, we've met before.

TURING. Have we? When?

PAT. You read a paper to the Moral Science Club at Cambridge. We met briefly afterwards.

TURING. That must've been — when? — six or seven years ago.

PAT. December, 1933. I remember it very clearly. I found your ideas tremendously exciting.

TURING. Thank you.

KNOX. *(to PAT:)* Have we found him somewhere to live?

PAT. The Crown Inn at Shenley Brook End.

KNOX. Oh good — that's only about three miles away. *(to TURING:)* Have you got a bicycle? You'll need a bicycle. *(to PAT:)* I shall rely on you to tell Mr. Turing about the Enigma.

PAT. Yes, of course.

KNOX. The point is, this damn code is a vital part of the Nazi war effort — vital. The army uses it, so does the Luftwaffe, and — most importantly — so do the U-boats. And if the U-boats get control of the north Atlantic, our merchant ships won't stand a chance. They'll starve us out. So — the Enigma has got to be broken. Somehow. Top priority.

TURING. What type of code is it? *(KNOX is gathering together his scattered papers and putting them back in the file.)*

PAT. Mechanical.

KNOX. Which puts the ball firmly in your court. But, first things first. Go back to Cambridge. Pack your bags. Pat will give you a guided tour on Monday morning. *(Picks up the file and goes to the door.)* Bletchley was chosen by the G.C.C.S. because it's equidistant from Oxford and Cambridge. I should warn you that the unexpected influx of academics and intellectuals has put a severe strain on local resources. You'll find it very difficult to get copies of *The Times* — or pipe tobacco. *(KNOX Exits. PAT follows him to the door.)*

PAT. I'll see you on Monday. *(Starts out.)*

TURING. Wait, um — can you tell me — in what way is the Enigma mechanical?

PAT. *(Closes door.)* The code is created by a machine rather like a typewriter; behind the keyboard are three rotors; the letters of the alphabet circle each rotor; and behind the rotors is a display board. If the operator presses a key — say the letter "A" — with the rotors in a specified position, a connection is made with, for example, the letter "D" and a bulb lights up on the output display over the letter "D."

TURING. The plain-text "A" is encoded into "D."

PAT. Yes — with the rotors in that chosen position. The first rotor then moves on. Pressing "A" might now produce a "P" or an "H" on the output display. When the rotor has made a complete revolution, the second does the same, and then the third. It's a polyalphabetical machine with 26 times 26 times 26 possible settings.

TURING. 17,576. Not a tremendously large number.

PAT. No, that's true. Manual analysis eventually leads to the correct setting, but it could take several days, and the setting is changed each day. The Germans use a codebook to indicate the setting — we haven't got one, of course. But at least we know how the thing works — and we've been able to build a machine tht simulates the Enigma's function, which is logical, symmetrical, self-inverse.

TURING. The sender and the receiver have the same equipment.

PAT. Yes. The trouble is, the Germans have just made the Enigma much more elaborate, which means that our machine is virtually obsolete. Their operators are now equipped with a stock of five rotors from which any three can be used in any order when they set up the Enigma.

TURING. 60 possible combinations! 17.576 times 60!

PAT. 1,054,560. They've also added a plugboard to the apparatus — like a telephone switchboard. They just connect pairs of letters with jackplugs and this swaps the letters before they're fed into the rotors — and after. So there are literally thousands of millions of possible permutations; and that's the problem; the basic problem, anyway; the Enigma they use in the U-boats is even more complicated. *(a grin)* Well, I'll see you on Monday.

TURING. Yes ... er, fine. I'll look forward to it. *(PAT Exits.)*

Scene 6

SCENE: LIGHTING change. Winter morning.

AT RISE: TURING takes off his jacket and puts on a dressing gown. RON Enters, wearing only trousers and a vest.

Ron. What's the time?

Turing. Nine o'clock.

Ron. *(RON yawns.)* Bit of a bloody mess.

Turing. What is?

Ron. This house. What's all that stuff in the bathroom? Doesn't half stink.

Turing. I'm trying to make some weedkiller.

Ron. What for?

Turing. To kill weeds.

Ron. Why don't you buy some? You could afford it.

Turing. I like making things. It's fun. Did you sleep all right?

Ron. Not bad. *(Pause; he looks at TURING.)* Do you often do this?

Turing. Do what?

Ron. Have blokes back here.

Turing. Not often.

Ron. Have you always been queer?

Turing. Yes.

Ron. Never fancied girls?

TURING. No.

RON. I like a bit of both, myself. I'd rather have a girl, given the chance, but they're not so easy to get, not when you're broke. *(pause)* Some real old queen picked me up when I was in London. Silk sheets, mirror over the bed. A bit different to this place. *(RON grins.)*

TURING. You were talking in your sleep.

RON. Was I? What did I say?

TURING. I couldn't make it out. You seemed frightened of something.

RON. I was having a dream. It's funny: I've had the same dream over and over again, ever since I was a kid.

TURING. What is it?

RON. Well, it's more of a nightmare, really. It's as if I'm in some huge empty space; sort of floating there, you know, just floating in mid-air in this great dark empty space. And suddenly, ever so quiet at first, a strange noise begins. Can't describe it. It's the sort of noise you can feel all through your body, and I start trembling. I can feel myself trembling with the noise, and as the noise gets louder, I tremble more and more and start to shake and it gets louder and louder, and there's nothing I can do to stop it, nothing. *(pause)*

TURING. What happens then?

RON. That's it. Then I wake up. *(grins)* Pretty spooky, eh? *(no response)* You don't half snore.

TURING. Sorry.

RON. Just like my dad. You can hear him snoring all over the bloody house.

TURING. What were you doing in London?

RON. How do you mean?

TURING. Were you working, having a holiday, or what?

RON. Sort of holiday, I suppose. I tried to get a job down there but nothing worked out. *(brief pause)* I got nicked pinching food from a Woolworth's. They sent me back here on probation. *(No response; pause.)* What's that place down the road?

TURING. What place?

RON. That big shed. You can see it from the bedroom window.

TURING. It's an old air-force hangar.

RON. I didn't know the R.A.F. was up here.

TURING. They were during the war.

RON. Were you here then?

TURING. No.

RON. Where were you?

TURING. Around and about.

RON. Doing what?

TURING. Working for the government.

RON. Doing what?

TURING. This and that.

RON. *(coaxing)* Tell me.

TURING. Can't. I promised not to.

RON. Promised who?

TURING. Mr. Churchill.

RON. I know ... you were making secret weapons.

TURING. In a way.

RON. *(intrigued)* Really?

TURING. *(playfully)* If it hadn't been for me, we'd have lost the war.

RON. *(grinning, skeptical)* Oh yeah?

TURING. Absolutely. *(quickly changing the subject)* I'll tell you something else.

RON. What's that?

TURING. That, um — that hangar down the road: it grows bigger at night.

RON. Bigger...?!

TURING. It's true. You look.

RON. *(a grin)* Don't be daft.

TURING. It seems to, anyway. In the daytime, it's just an ordinary large shed, but when the sun goes down it seems to get bigger and bigger. I'm thinking of writing a story about it.

RON. *(playing along)* Good idea.

TURING. Do you think so?

RON. Why not?

TURING. It's rather like that film you enjoyed so much.

RON. The one about the robot?

TURING. Yes. It's quite creepy, quite spooky. I imagine that I go inside the hangar; it's deserted, derelict, very dark — you can't see a thing. And as I go in, the door bangs shut behind me.

RON. No way out.

TURING. No way out. Then — then I realize that it's not a hangar at all. I'm trapped inside an enormous mechanical brain. And this brain, the hangar, starts to play chess with me. And I've got to win, otherwise I'll never get out. All day and all night, we play; all the next day and all the next night. But the brain's too clever for me, I can't keep up with the moves — and I'm terrified

I'll be trapped in there for the rest of my life. *(brief pause)* The trouble is, I can't think of a good ending.

RON. Flash Gordon comes in and rescues you.

TURING. *(smiles)* I thought perhaps I could find a piece of chalk and write a few sums on the wall: very easy sums, simple arithmetic, that sort of thing; and I'd do them deliberately badly, make silly mistakes; I'd do them so slowly and so badly that the brain would get more and more despairing and then, finally—

RON. What?

TURING. The brain commits suicide. What do you think of that?

RON. Flash Gordon's better.

TURING. *(a smile)* Maybe.

RON. *(Stands up.)* Got any tea?

TURING. In the kitchen. *(RON Exits.)*

RON. *(offstage)* There's no milk.

TURING. Sorry. *(RON returns.)*

RON. No tea either, just coffee.

TURING. We'll have some breakfast later.

RON. I'm starving. Aren't there any shops around here?

TURING. There's a place at the end of the road.

RON. I'll run down, shall I? Got any money?

TURING. Put your clothes on, I'll find some money.

RON. Right. *(RON Exits. TURING takes his wallet from his jacket pocket; he is clearly surprised by what he finds inside; he recounts the bank notes, checking them carefully. RON Enters, now wearing a sweater and a windcheater.)* I'll get some tea and milk. How about some bacon?

TURING. Have you been taking money from my wallet?

RON. What?

TURING. You heard.

RON. I haven't touched your bloody wallet.

TURING. I had fifteen pounds in here yesterday, there's only seven left.

RON. It's nothing to do with me.

TURING. Where's it gone then?

RON. How should I know?

TURING. Come on, give it back.

RON. I haven't got it!

TURING. I don't believe you.

RON. All right, search me—

TURING. Don't be ridiculous.

RON. — come on, search me.

TURING. You've hidden it somewhere.

RON. What the fuck are you talking about? *(Brief pause; TURING and RON stand facing each other.)* Why should I take money from you?

TURING. You said you were hard up.

RON. I didn't.

TURING. You said you were out of work.

RON. So what?

TURING. Please, Ron, give it back.

RON. Piss off!

TURING. Give it back and we'll say no more about it.

RON. I'm not a bloody thief!

TURING. You just said you were. You said you're on probation.

RON. If you think I pinched that money, call the police. *(TURING does not move.)* Come on, there's the phone — what are you waiting for? *(Grabs the telephone receiver.)* Come on!

TURING. Put it down. *(RON throws the telephone receiver onto the floor and strides angrily across the room; TURING stands motionless, looking at him.)* I'm sorry. I'm sorry. *(Picks up the receiver and replaces it on the telephone.)* I lost my temper. I'm sorry. *(no response)* Perhaps I made a mistake.

RON. Fucking nerve!

TURING. I'm sorry. *(RON goes to the door.)* Where are you going?

RON. I'm not bloody staying here.

TURING. Please don't go.

RON. *(girlish, mocking him)* Please don't go.

TURING. I must've been mistaken. *(no response)* I thought I had fifteen pounds. Perhaps I didn't. Let's forget about it. *(Takes some money from his wallet.)* Go and get us some breakfast.

RON. *(Mimicking him.)* G-g-get it yourself.

TURING. I've said I'm sorry.

RON. So what?

TURING. Let's be friends. *(Pause; TURING takes a step toward RON.)* Do you want some money? Do you? *(RON almost replies; hesitates.)* How much do you need?

RON. I'm not a bloody renter.

TURING. I know. *(brief pause)* If you're hard up, if you want some money, you've only got to ask. *(brief pause)*

RON. Call it a loan, then.

TURING. How much?

RON. Three? *(TURING takes three pound notes from his wallet and gives them to RON.)*

TURING. Shall I see you again?

Ron. Maybe. Yeah, maybe.

Turing. Perhaps I'll see you down the pub.

Ron. Yeah. *(brief pause)* I'd better go.

Turing. Have some breakfast first. Tea and bacon. *(Offers more money for food.)* Have some breakfast, then go. I'll cook you bacon and eggs. *(RON hesitates.)*

Ron. I can't stay long.

Turing. I know.

Ron. Okay. *(Takes the money.)* Where's this shop? Down the road?

Turing. Down the road, turn left. *(RON Exits.)*

Scene 7

SCENE: LIGHTING change: Summer afternoon; shadows of foliage.

AT RISE: SARA and PAT Enter; they are wearing summer clothes. SARA is carrying a tray with a jug and two glasses; she puts the tray on a table; PAT is holding a glass.

Sara. There are no oranges and no lemons, so we've made a fruit cocktail out of apples and pears.

Pat. It tastes very nice.

Turing. It's a depressing color.

Sara. Don't keep finding fault. Things are difficult enough these days. *(Pours the drink.)* Pat's coming to church with me.

TURING. Oh good.

SARA. *(giving a glass to TURING)* Do come, Alan, dear.

TURING. Not today. *(sipping the drink)* Ugh!

PAT. What's the matter?

TURING. It's terribly sour.

PAT. Is it?

TURING. Try some.

PAT. I already have.

SARA. *(to PAT.)* I'm so glad you were able to come down today. I was afraid there might've been a last minute change of plans.

PAT. I've been looking forward to it.

SARA. Have you, dear? So have I. It's so seldom that Alan invites his friends to see us. Hardly ever, in fact. Of course it was different when he was at school. His friend Chris used to come most holidays. Such a charming boy. And a very nice family.

TURING. I don't think Pat wants to hear about my boyhood friendships.

SARA. Why not? It's always interesting to learn something about people you're fond of. *(offering to refill PAT'S glass)* Would you like some more?

PAT. Please.

SARA. *(to TURING, as she pours the drink.)* Do come to church, Alan; it'd be so nice if we all went together.

TURING. What's the point?

SARA. Does there have to be a point?

TURING. It seems idiotic for a non-believer to spend his Sunday evening in church.

SARA. You're not a non-believer.

TURING. I am.

SARA. You used not to be. *(to PAT:)* He was once extremely devout.

TURING. You never understood what I thought.

SARA. *(briskly)* Maybe not. *(quickly addressing PAT)* I do envy your having gone to Cambridge. When I was young it was considered a waste of time to give a girl a good education. And if you did show any sign of intellectual ability, people seemed to regard you with a degree of suspicion — as if intelligence was somehow unfeminine and unattractive. It was really most unfair.

TURING. *(raising his glass)* This needs some sugar. Do you have any sugar?

SARA. We only get eight ounces a week — or doesn't rationing apply to people like you?

TURING. People like me?

SARA. One's always hearing about people in hush-hush jobs living off the fat of the land.

TURING. Ask Pat. *(to PAT:)* Would you say we lived off the fat of the land?

PAT. *(smiles)* Hardly.

TURING. Absolutely not. *(to SARA:)* And stop fishing.

SARA. Fishing...?

TURING. All these hints about hush-hush jobs; you know perfectly well we can't tell you what we do.

SARA. All right, don't be cross. *(Turns to leave.)* I'll go and see if we've got any sugar. *(SARA Exits.)*

PAT. She's quite right, you know.

TURING. What about?

PAT. I do like hearing about your family and friends. I wish you talked about them.

TURING. I do sometimes.

PAT. Apart from anything else, it's embarrassing. I had no idea your father was ill until your mother mentioned it.

TURING. He's not ill; he's in poor health. He had a prostate operation some years ago, and he's been vaguely off-color ever since. And my brother's in the army, by the way — just to complete the picture; he's in the army, in Egypt.

PAT. Yes, I know.

TURING. I suppose my mother told you.

PAT. Yes.

TURING. Since she's telling you everything, there's no need for me to duplicate the information. *(He looks at PAT; she says nothing.)* Well, is there?

PAT. Who's Chris?

TURING. Christopher was a friend of mine at Sherborne.

PAT. Your mother obviously liked him.

TURING. Yes. *(Pause; the irritation recedes.)* Yes — he was a remarkable boy. Very clever. Very perceptive. Very mature for his age. He made everyone else seem so ordinary. It was one of those intense friendships that only happen when you're young. I worshipped the ground he walked on. *(PAT looks at him; he seems anxious to avoid her gaze.)*

PAT. Have you kept in touch?

TURING. He died. *(brief pause)* He'd had T.B. when he was a small boy. I didn't know that. He never told me. He hadn't really recovered. He was taken ill at school. We were all asleep. The next morning I heard he'd been rushed to hospital. He died six days later. Thursday, February 13th, 1930. I was devastated. *(Pause. TURING sips his fruit drink.)*

PAT. Poor Alan.

TURING. *(TURING looks at her; a shy hesitation before he speaks.)* I felt ... I felt I should've died and not him; and that the only possible excuse for living was that I should achieve something Christopher could no longer do. *(brief pause)* I used to think ... after he died, I almost believed that he was still with me in spirit and could help me. *(a wry smile)* It was that, I think, that gave my mother the impression that I was devoutly religious. It wasn't that at all. I was obsessed with the idea — with the question — whether or not Christopher's mind could exist without his body. It was an obsession that stayed with me for many years. What are mental processes? Can they take place in something other than a living brain? In a way — in a very real way — many of the problems I've tried to solve in my work lead directly back to Christopher. *(smiles)* Wouldn't he be amused?

PAT. I think he'd be pleased.

TURING. I hope so. *(Pause. PAT touches his hand: a gentle, fleeting gesture.)*

PAT. Why don't you come to church? It'd give your mother so much pleasure.

TURING. It would be a lie. Like pretending this ghastly drink isn't ghastly. *(Puts the glass on the table.)* Ugh!

PAT. It's a pretty harmless pretense.

TURING. Most pretense is self-deluding, and that's far from harmless. *(animated)* Just look at all our confrères at Bletchley — everyone pretending to be so radiantly optimistic! Why do it — why? What's the point?

PAT. It's better than being gloomy all the time.

TURING. Is it? *(brief pause)* I worked out the chances of our being able to crack the U-boat Enigma. Guess what they are.

PAT. Well, I suppose it must be something like—

TURING. *(cutting in)* Fifty-thousand-to-one against.

PAT. Perhaps we'll capture a codebook.

TURING. Unlikely. My faith in the Admiralty is nil.

PAT. We might be lucky.

TURING. Pigs might fly. *(brief pause)* And I've been wondering what would happen if we lost the war — how we'd survive.

PAT. Don't think about such things.

TURING. Come on now, we must — otherwise we're just burying our heads in the sand.

PAT. All we can do is live from day to day; everything changes, you know that.

TURING. We ought to make plans.

PAT. Like what?

TURING. Well, I thought of buying some razor blades.

PAT. Razor blades?

TURING. They'll be in very short supply if we lose the war, so at least we'd have something to sell.

PAT. *(Stares at him.)* How many razor blades?

TURING. Enough to fill a large suitcase.

PAT. *(laughing)* Oh, Prof — you're not serious.

TURING. I certainly am.

PAT. You can't just walk into a chemist's shop and buy hundreds — thousands — of razor blades. *(no response)* Well, can you?

TURING. I don't know. Possibly.

PAT. Well, you can't. *(brief pause)*

TURING. I could buy some silver.

PAT. Silver what?

TURING. Lumps of it — ingots, or whatever they're called. If I took some money out of the bank and bought a couple of silver ingots, I could bury them and dig them up when the war is over.

PAT. Bury them where?

TURING. Anywhere — somewhere at Bletchley.

PAT. *(laughing)* Oh, Alan...!

TURING. Why not? I'm serious, I mean it — I've already made some enquiries about buying the silver. *(PAT'S laughter fades; she is moved by his boyish earnestness; she reaches out and takes him by the hand.)*

PAT. *(tenderly)* Oh, Alan ... *(Disturbed by this show of intimacy, TURING turns from her abruptly and plunges his hand into his pocket; he pulls out a fir cone.)*

TURING. Look at this. It's a fir cone.

PAT. I can see it's a fir cone.

TURING. Take it. Look at it. *(She does so.)* I'll tell you something extraordinary about it.

PAT. It looks ordinary enough to me.

TURING. Define what is meant by a Fibonacci sequence.

PAT. A Fibonacci sequence is a sequence of numbers where each is the sum of the previous two; you start with one and one—then one plus one equals two—one and two, three—two and three, five—three and five, eight—

TURING. *(continuing the sequence)* —five and eight, thirteen. Well done, full marks. Now look at that fir cone. Look at the pattern of the bracts — the leaves. Follow them spiralling round the cone: eight lines twisting round to the left, thirteen twisting to the right. The numbers always come from the Fibonacci sequence.

PAT. *(examining the fir cone more closely)* Always...?

TURING. Always. And it's not just fir cones — the petals of most flowers grow in the same way. Isn't that amazing?

PAT. Yes, it is.

TURING. And it prompts the age-old question: is God a mathematician? *(TURING smiles; PAT looks at him; she returns the fir cone.)*

PAT. I love you, Prof. *(no response)* I love you. You know that.

TURING. Yes.

PAT. You're supposed to say "I love you too."

TURING. I know. *(pause)*

PAT. Please say something.

TURING. I don't think of myself as a very lovable person.

PAT. Well you are.

TURING. There are lots of men at Bletchley who are much more lovable than I am.

PAT. That's where you're wrong.

TURING. Don't be silly, of course there are, I see them every lunchtime, rushing around, laughing, playing cricket. I'm amazed you haven't fallen in love with one of them.

PAT. Because they're dull, that's why.

TURING. So am I.

PAT. That's where you're wrong. You're untidy and messy and lacking almost all the social graces; your clothes are stained and you bite your nails; you tell the truth when it would be kinder to tell a lie, and you've got no patience with people who bore you. But you are not dull. And I love you. *(pause)*

TURING. As a matter of fact, I do love you.

PAT. *(not really a question)* As a friend.

TURING. As a friend.

PAT. That might change. *(a sad smile)* Perhaps it might change. *(TURING goes to PAT and takes her by the hand.)*

TURING. I'm a homosexual.

PAT. I know. That doesn't stop me loving you. It needn't stop you loving me.

TURING. It would stop me making love to you. I don't want that sort of life and I don't think you do, either.

(SARA Enters, carrying a bowl of sugar; seeing TURING and PAT, standing so intimately together, she immediately freezes.)

SARA. Oh, I'm sorry. *(TURING and PAT spring apart.)*

TURING. *(going to SARA)* Don't bother with the sugar. That drink is undrinkable. I'll make some tea, shall I? Would you like some tea? *(He takes the sugar bowl from SARA.)* Give me that. *(To PAT.)* Tea or sherry, which would you prefer?

PAT. I don't mind.

TURING. If you're going to church, it had better be tea. We don't want you breathing alcoholic fumes all over the vicar. *(TURING Exits. PAT stands very still, her head bowed; SARA looks at her anxiously.)*

SARA. What's the matter?

PAT. Nothing.

SARA. Has Alan said something to upset you?

PAT. No, of course not.

SARA. Sorry. It's none of my business. I'm sorry. *(PAT attempts a reassuring smile.)*

PAT. Nothing's wrong. Everything's perfectly all right. *(SARA sighs.)*

SARA. He's always been his own worst enemy, always. Even when he was young, even at school. His headmaster at Sherborne called him anti-social, I remember. We were very upset. *(PAT can think of no appropriate response; she turns from SARA.)*

PAT. I'd better get ready for church.

SARA. Don't come if you don't want to.

PAT. No, I'd like to, really. *(Picks up the tray of glasses.)* I'll take this, shall I?

SARA. Thank you. *(PAT Exits; again SARA sighs; then she follows PAT.)*

Scene 8

SCENE: LIGHTING change: Winter morning.

AT RISE: The rat-a-tat-tat of a front door knocker.

> *TURING Enters; he is wearing running shorts and a singlet; he opens a door; ROSS Enters.*

TURING. *(some surprise)* Sergeant Ross.

Ross. Sorry to bother you at home, sir.

Turing. It's no bother. Please come in.

Ross. Thank you, sir. *(TURING closes the door; he feels obliged to explain his mode of dress.)*

Turing. I've just been, uh ... I do a bit of running.

Ross. Ah.

Turing. I can't do as much as I used to, alas. *(small smile)* Middle-age creeping on.

Ross. What were you: long distance, sprinter or what?

Turing. Long distance. Marathon, actually.

Ross. God, I couldn't run that far when I was twenty, let alone now. *(TURING smiles; he and ROSS stand facing each other.)*

Turing. Do you, um ... do you want to ask me some more question?

Ross. Yes, sir, I do; but first of all, I think we should try to clear up this story of yours.

Turing. What story?

Ross. The one about a young man coming to your house to sell things; brushes, I think you said...?

Turing. Yes?

Ross. We have good reason to believe that you were lying. *(no response)* Were you lying?

Turing. *(hesitates)* Yes.

Ross. Why?

Turing. I'm sorry. It was very foolish of me.

Ross. Would you like to tell me what really happened?

Turing. There was no brush salesman. I, uh ... a friend told me about the burglar. George.

Ross. A friend...?

TURING. Yes.

ROSS. How did this friend know about the burglary?

TURING. He didn't know, exactly; he guessed.

ROSS. How did he guess?

TURING. He was having a drink with George, you see; in a milk bar, and, uh ... he mentioned me, my friend mentioned me, and told George where I lived. *(ROSS looks; waits.)* He'd been to dinner, you see. My friend. He'd been to dinner just a few days before, and he was telling George all about it. And then, um ... after the burglary — I told my friend what had happened and he said it might've been George. He knew that George was a petty thief, or whatever the expression is. It was just a guess.

ROSS. Well, your friend was right.

TURING. Was he?

ROSS. Detectives found some fingerprints here in your house. This man George has a criminal record.

TURING. Oh, I see. So that proves it? *(no response)* Yes, I see. *(brief pause)*

ROSS. This friend of yours: what's his name?

TURING. Ron. Ron Miller.

ROSS. A colleague of yours at the university?

TURING. Well, no.

ROSS. A social acquaintance?

TURING. In a way.

ROSS. Have you known him long?

TURING. Not long.

ROSS. How long?

TURING. Three or four weeks.

ROSS. And in those three or four weeks, how many

times have you seen him?

TURING. About once a week.

ROSS. How did you meet?

TURING. Just — you know, casually.

ROSS. He's just a casual, social acquaintance?

TURING. Yes.

ROSS. Not what you'd call a close friend?

TURING. Oh no.

ROSS. So why did you lie to conceal his identity?

TURING. I, um ... I didn't want to get him into trouble.

ROSS. Why not?

TURING. Well...

ROSS. He was, after all, partly responsible for your house being burgled.

TURING. I wouldn't say that.

ROSS. Wouldn't you, sir?

TURING. I wouldn't say, responsible.

ROSS. Partly responsible.

TURING. It's difficult to say. I mean, it's difficult to say exactly what his involvement in all this actually was — is.

ROSS. He told George your address.

TURING. Yes.

ROSS. And presumably he knows that George has got a criminal record.

TURING. Well, yes.

ROSS. So why go to all these lengths to protect him?

TURING. *(blurting it out)* The truth is, I'm having an affair with him. *(pause)*

Ross. With Miller?

Turing. With Ron, yes.

Ross. You're having a sexual relationship with this man?

Turing. Yes.

Ross. What sort of sexual relationship?

Turing. How many sorts are there?

Ross. You tell me, sir.

Turing. What exactly do you want to know?

Ross. I need to understand the precise nature of this sexual relationship.

Turing. You mean you want to know what we did?

Ross. That would help.

Turing. Well — since you ask — it wasn't much more than mutual masturbation.

Ross. Did penetration occur?

Turing. No.

Ross. You do realize, don't you, sir, that this is a criminal offense?

Turing. Look, isn't this rather beside the point? I thought we were trying to establish who had burgled my house.

Ross. That's part of it, yes.

Turing. "Part of it" ... ? Part of what?

Ross. You've just told me that you've committed a criminal offense. I can't ignore that, can I?

Turing. What criminal offense?

Ross. Gross indecency.

Turing. Oh, now look — I didn't corrupt him — Ron knew what he was doing — he came to my house — *my* house, don't forget — he came here perfectly well aware that we'd almost certainly go to bed together — it didn't come as any great surprise to him — he'd had other homosexual experiences — I mean, it's ludicrous to talk about criminal offenses — and, as I say, everything happened here, in private, in my own house, in private — if I hadn't told you, you wouldn't have known anything about it.

Ross. But you did tell me.

Turing. Can't you forget about it? *(no response)* Can't you? *(pause)*

Ross. How old is this man, Miller?

Turing. I don't know. Nineteen, twenty.

Ross. And how old are you, sir?

Turing. Thirty-nine. *(brief pause)* Obviously I shouldn't have told you. I'm always saying things I shouldn't say. *(no response)* Look — surely there's no need to make a fuss about this? I mean, surely you can forget what I told you. Can't you? It's not asking much, after all. Please. *(ROSS remains silent; pause.)* What's the position if I make a statement? Shall I?

Ross. That's up to you, sir. *(TURING hesitates for a moment.)*

Turing. Anyway ... all right ... yes, I'll make a statement. *(Looks at ROSS.)* You'll want me to go to the police station. I'd better get dressed. *(TURING Exits briskly.)*

CURTAIN

ACT II
Scene 1

TURING. Mr. Headmaster, members of the staff, boys. I want you to imagine a bowl of porridge. A bowl of cold porridge. When I was a boy here at Sherborne — some twenty-five years ago — we always had porridge for breakfast — every day, winter and summer — or so it seems. And for some unaccountable reason, by the time the porridge reached me it was always cold. My friend, Christopher Morcom, was more fortunate; he enjoyed his porridge and ate it heartily. But I sat there every morning staring miserably into my bowl of cold porridge: all grey and soft and wrinkled on top. You must be wondering why I'm telling you this. Your Headmaster has asked me here to talk about my work with computers and here I am describing bowls of cold porridge. Well, there's a very good reason for it and I'll come to that in a moment. I daresay the word "computer" is unfamiliar to many of you. It is to lots of people. But if I were to say Electronic Brain — ah! — that's much more interesting. And if I were to ask, can a machine think? — I'm sure you'd all be intrigued to know the answer. But before we can consider that question properly, I must tell you something about computers and how they work. First of all, let me compare a computer with the human brain — which brings us back to our bowl of porridge, because that's what the human brain looks like: same color, same texture. A computer is very different. It's big — the size of several large wardrobes all joined together; it's hard and metallic on the outside, terribly complicated inside, with lots of valves and condensers and so on — not a bit like cold porridge, but that doesn't matter. It's the logical pattern of the brain that counts, not the grey stuff it's made of. The same with a computer. What matters is its logic. And the logic of a computer is really very simple. All it does is to read a list of instructions — we call this a program — which it then carries out methodically. And the only thing you have to do is to write down exactly what you want done in a language the computer understands. I know this may sound like a fanciful theory, but I assure you that it's not. The computer we've built at Manchester University has been working for over four years, since 1949, and in that time it has successfully tackled a wide variety of tasks. People assume that computers are just glorified calculating machines. Not so. It's true that computers are often used to do calculating because they do calculate very quickly — but computer programs don't have to have aything to do with numbers. A colleague of mine has got our computer to hum tunes — it once sang "Jingle Bells." We've even got it to write love letters! So — doing calculations, humming tunes, writing love letters. All very different tasks, but all performed by one machine. And that's an extremely important fact about computers. A computer is a universal machine. It can perform any task that can be described in symbols. Now

many people think that a computer can only do what it's
been told to do. Well, it's true that we may start off like
that — but it's only the start. A computer can be made to
learn. Suppose, for example, that it was set to play chess.
It could find out for itself, in the light of its own experience,
which were winning and which were losing strategies,
and then drop the losing ones. After a while we wouldn't
know which instructions it was actually using; so it would
hardly be fair to say that we had instructed it what to do.
That would be like crediting the master with any
originality shown by the pupil. The question thus arises
as to whether or not we would credit such a machine with
intelligence. I would say that we must. It is my view that a
computer being a universal machine, can perform any
task that the human brain can carry out. Any task. What I
would very much like to do is to educate a computer, partly
by direct training, partly by letting it find out things for
itself. We don't know how to do this yet, but I believe that
it will be achieved in the very near future — and I feel
sure that by the year 2000, it will be considered perfectly
correct to speak of an intelligent machine or to say that a
computer is thinking. Of course not everyone agrees with
this view, far from it. There are those who say that thinking is a function of man's immortal soul and since a
machine has no soul it cannot think. Surely this is
blasphemous — who are we to deny the possibility that
God may wish to grant a soul to a machine? Then there is
what I call the "Heads in the Sand" objection. "The consequences of machines thinking is too dreadful to con-
template," people say "such a thing could never
happen." This point of view is usually expressed by

intellectuals. They have the most to lose. Another objection — and this is one I hear very frequently — is that a machine cannot be said to think until it can write a sonnet or compose a concerto, feel grief when its valves fuse, be warmed by flattery, be angry or depressed when it can't get what it wants. Well, of course one might reply that there are precious few human beings who can write a sonnet or compose a concerto — and I can see no reason at all why a thinking machine should not be kind, resourceful, beautiful, friendly, have a sense of humor, tell right from wrong, make mistakes, fall in love, or enjoy strawberries and cream. At the moment such considerations should not concern us; but it might be rather nice — don't you think? — if, one day, we could find out just what a machine can *feel.*

Scene 2

SCENE: LIGHTING change: Autumn afternoon.

AT RISE: KNOX Enters, leaning heavily on a stick.

KNOX. Did I tell you what happened to my brother?
TURING. *(at table, looking thru papers)* What was that?
KNOX. They were having a dinner party. It was some time ago, during the blitz. Eddie was just about to open a bottle of claret when a bomb fell nearby. Tremendous explosion. Bang! Guess what happened.

TURING. I've no idea.

KNOX. The blast was so severe that the cork shot straight out of the bottle. Isn't that amazing? Eddie, of course, was quite unperturbed. "If only one could rely on its happening regularly," he said. *(KNOX and TURING laugh; then KNOX frowns.)* Why did I tell you that? There was something on my mind. What was it? *(ponders)* Damn. My memory's hopeless these days. I have to write everything down. *(smiles)* Old age, that's the trouble. We all live far too long. My solicitor says that dentists are to blame.

TURING. Yes, you told me.

KNOX. Did I? Ah. *(brief pause)* Have you been to London recently?

TURING. No, not for ages.

KNOX. The bomb damage is frightful. Rose Macaulay says that walking through St. John's Wood is like walking through the ruins of Babylon and Pompeii. *(a sudden thought)* I know why I told you that story: dinner party — bottle of claret. *(Opens a drawer and takes out a bottle of whisky.)* — real scotch! Would you like some?

TURING. Not for me, thank you.

KNOX. No...?

TURING. No, I don't like it.

KNOX. Don't you? Neither do I. Isn't that a shame? Somebody gave it to me. Very nice of them. Ah, well — never mind. *(Replaces the bottle.)* I thought we should have a drink in honor of your trip to Washington.

TURING. I'm not going just yet.

KNOX. It's all settled, though?

TURING. So I believe.

KNOX. Well, sooner you than me. From what I know about the Americans — which isn't very much — they'll spend most of the time trying to persuade you that we're doing everything wrong, and that their methods are infinitely superior.

TURING. Be that as it may — Their ships are being sunk all over the place and it's given them a big shock. They've demanded access to our methods — and I've got to go. *(wry smile)* Let's hope the U-boats don't sink me first. And it's not all one-sided; they're prepared to tell me about their work on speech encipherment ... Tremendously important. It's simply horrifying that all communications across the Atlantic have to go by short-wave radio. Anyone can listen.

KNOX. Speech scramblers...?

TURING. *(dismissively)* Come on, they're easily penetrated. What's needed is an unbreakable speech encipherment system. But one doesn't exist. *(small smile)* Not yet anyway.

KNOX. *(Smiles; brief pause.)* It's important that you're going.

TURING. Yes, it is.

KNOX. I mean it's important that it's you who are going and not some more conventional representative.

TURING. At least I know what I'm talking about.

KNOX. And you're going with your friend Churchill's personal authority.

TURING. Yes.

KNOX. That's important, too. We're not very popular with the bureaucrats or the brass-hats. *Au contraire.* The fact that you're the one who's going to Washington is very significant.

TURING. I think that's mostly Churchill's doing.

KNOX. Oh, I'm sure of it. He knows how vital your work is. "The geese who lay the golden eggs;" isn't that what he said?

TURING. He meant all of us.

KNOX. You in particular. *(TURING glances at KNOX.)*

TURING. This is all very flattering, Knox. You're making me feel uneasy.

KNOX. Why is that?

TURING. I sense a sting in the tail approaching.

KNOX. Not a sting exactly. *(briefest pause)* I gather you've been chaining your tea mug to the radiator.

TURING. Not an unreasonable precaution. Tea mugs are in short supply.

KNOX. Some people find it irritating.

TURING. I find it irritating that some people should be irritated.

KNOX. *(sighs)* I've come to the conclusion that the old cliché about eccentric artists is inaccurate. Scientists carry eccentricity to far greater lengths. *(a glance at a silent TURING)* Not just you — others — your friend Wittgenstein, for example.

TURING. Wittgenstein is not a scientist.

KNOX. Philosopher, then; mathematician — does it matter? Even you must agree that he's dauntingly eccentric. And rude. *(no response)* A friend of mine took me to meet him. There he was, this distinguished Fellow of Trinity, sitting in a deck-chair in a completely bare room. My friend introduced me and said that I would be interested in attending one of his classes. Wittgenstein looked at me with those cold, piercing eyes. "My lectures are not for tourists," he said.

TURING. *(a shrug)* He lives life as he chooses. What's wrong with that? *(brief pause)*

KNOX. I do think you ought to be a little more discreet.

TURING. About my tea mug?

KNOX. About this young engineer chap you've got working with you. Tongues are beginning to wag.

TURING. *(Stares at him.)* Am I in for a lesson in morals?

KNOX. In common sense. I don't give a tuppenny damn whether you choose to go to bed with choirboys or cocker spaniels, but it would be wiser to keep your private life to yourself.

TURING. Is this an official reprimand?

KNOX. Friendly advice, nothing more. *(trying to adopt a more relaxed tone)* I mean, first things first: let's get our priorities right. What we're doing here — and most especially what you're doing here — has a direct and crucial bearing on the progress of the war. A pretty young engineer comes a rather poor second to that, surely?

TURING. Nobody complained when I was working with Pat.

KNOX. That was different.

TURING. Was it?

KNOX. Of course it was.

TURING. I thought you said rules only mattered in cricket.

KNOX. *(irritably)* Oh, it's such nonsense, this contemporary obsession with sexual fulfillment! Passion is dreadfully overrated, if you ask me. One is happiest when sex is a dimly remembered pleasure, like building sandcastles or climbing apple trees.

TURING. You can hardly expect me to agree with that.

KNOX. Like all of us, I can only speak from personal experience. I have been happily married for over twenty years, and I'm glad to say that passion has never played a significant rôle in our relationship. Understanding and companionship can be relied upon. Passion is forever fleeting.

TURING. Does that really matter?

KNOX. It matters to me.

TURING. Perhaps one brief moment of passion is worth more than twenty years of uneventful companionship.

KNOX. I didn't say it was uneventful. Anyway, we're not talking about me, we're talking about you.

TURING. I hear you're not very well.

KNOX. What's that got to do with it?

TURING. Nothing. I was changing the subject.

KNOX. *(ignoring this)* A great many people — administrators and the military alike — regard Bletchley as a hotbed of anarchy and unruliness. They pray for an excuse to bring us to heel.

TURING. *(furious)* The bureaucrats and the military should be bloody grateful to have me here!

KNOX. Most of them have spent their lives in a world of rigid discipline: rank, routine, procedure — that's all they know. Then you come along: work then you feel like

it, complain about this, that and the other; ignore what
few rules we do have here — and what's more, what's
worse, you get away with it. You succeed. Can you blame
them for disliking you?

TURING. They're small-minded. Petty. Spiteful.

KNOX. Well, maybe.

TURING. What's the point of having a system that gives
authority to people who don't deserve it? You say I complained — good God, of course I complained! — nothing
was being done — you know that as well as I do. Nobody
understood the *scale* of the problem — it wasn't just a
question of more staff and more money — we needed
new ideas, electronics: an industry! — and absolutely
bugger-all was being done about it. If I hadn't written to
Mr. Churchill — if I'd gone through the so-called proper
channels — we'd all be stuck here, twiddling our thumbs
and getting nowhere fast. *(KNOX tries to reply, but TURING
is not to be silenced.)* Do these people know how Churchill
replied to my letter? Do they? "Make sure they have all
they want on extreme priority," that's what he said.

KNOX. I know.

TURING. "Action this day!"

KNOX. Yes, I know — and I'm not saying you did the
wrong thing: I'm just trying to explain why such
unorthodox methods are bound to cause a consider-
able upset.

TURING. All that matters is the work we do. Differences
of attitude, differences of personality, shouldn't come
into it.

KNOX. They shouldn't, but they do.

TURING. Then they should be ignored.

Knox. I think not.

Turing. Well, I do.

Knox. You can't go through life ignoring the effect you have on other people or the effect that other people have on you.

Turing. *(deliberately provocative)* You can try.

Knox. You've spent far too much time thinking about your Turing machines. We are, after all, human beings; and you should try to accept the many imperfections that are part of our human condition.

Turing. Tolerate, perhaps; not accept.

Knox. Nevertheless, allowances have to be made; compromises have to be reached.

Turing. I beg to differ.

Knox. All right! — let me give you an example. A few minutes ago, you enquired about my health. Suppose I had answered you directly. Suppose I had told you that I am mortally ill and have only a year or so to live. Suppose I had broken down and wept. Suppose I had opened my heart to you and said that I had no wish to die; that I was frightened and in despair. I can't believe that you would have welcomed such a disclosure. I feel sure that you'd have found it distressing, embarrassing and somewhat inconsiderate. And so — being aware of your feelings as well as my own — it would seem to be both correct and appropriate for me to moderate my response.

Turing. Are you dying?

Knox. Similarly — or so it seems to me — when you reveal the nature of your sexuality, you cannot afford to ignore the effect it's bound to have on other people. Fear, for example; when people are asked to accept something they do not understand. Or anger — when what you so unashamedly reveal seems to be contrary to everything they've ever believed in. And pain. You're bound to cause a lot of pain. Not for yourself, necessarily — that's your concern, anyway — but for people who are close to you, anyone who's fond of you. Pain. Real pain. *(TURING is silent; brief pause.)* Speaking of Wittgenstein; he once wrote something that impressed me deeply. I sat down, there and then with the book in my hand, and memorized what he had written. This is what he said: "We feel that even when all possible scientific questions have been answered, the problems of life remain completely unanswered." *(KNOX Exits.)*

Scene 3

SCENE: LIGHTING change: Crisp winter's day.

AT RISE: SARA Enters and goes to TURING.

SARA. Alan, my dear, you are so silly! *(She embraces him.)* Why didn't you tell me you were coming down?

TURING. I wasn't sure I'd be able to make it. I didn't want to disappoint you.

SARA. Well, it's a wonderful surprise. I'm delighted. *(another embrace)* Just look at that dreadful jacket. I do wish you'd take more care of yourself. How long can you stay? Don't tell me you've got to go rushing back tomorrow morning.

TURING. I may have to.

SARA. Never mind, don't let's think about that. I've had the guest room completely redecorated — dreadfully expensive, but worth every penny.

TURING. Mother, listen — I've got something to tell you.

SARA. *(Looks at him: a sudden intuition of bad news.)* Something nice?

TURING. I'm afraid not.

SARA. *(Turns from him, not wishing to look at his face.)* No, you wouldn't have come all this way to tell me anything nice. What is it?

TURING. Well, I ... I'm in trouble.

SARA. What sort of trouble?

TURING. Serious trouble.

SARA. Tell me. *(TURING opens his mouth to speak, but cannot find the words.)*

TURING. It's so difficult to explain.

SARA. *(trying to help)* Is it something to do with money?

TURING. No. *(struggling to tell her)* Look — you know I've never been very interested in women.

SARA. People of your sort seldom are.

TURING. *(Has she guessed the truth?)* My sort ... ? What do you mean, my sort?

SARA. People who spend their lives with their heads buried in books.

TURING. It's nothing to do with that.

SARA. What, then?

TURING. I've no sexual feeling for women.

SARA. That's probably just as well. People seem to be

getting divorced at such a rate these days.

TURING. Please listen. Please try to understand.

SARA. I'm doing my best.

TURING. The police have discovered that I'm having an affair with a boy. *(Pause; SARA stares at him.)*

SARA. A boy?

TURING. I'm sorry. There's no other way to tell you.

SARA. *(Stares at him.)* A *boy...?*

TURING. I'm sorry.

SARA. Have you told your brother?

TURING. Yes.

SARA. What did he say?

TURING. Shocked. Terribly shocked.

SARA. Have you always been like this?

TURING. Yes.

SARA. Always?

TURING. Yes.

SARA. But what about that girl you were engaged to? What was her name? Pat.

TURING. I was never engaged to her.

SARA. I thought you loved her.

TURING. I was fond of her. I loved her as a friend.

SARA. Will this affect your career?

TURING. I suppose so.

SARA. How?

TURING. I don't know.

SARA. What's going to happen?

TURING. Well, uh ... there'll be a trial.

SARA. They're sending you to court?

TURING. Yes.

SARA. When?

TURING. Soon. March. The end of March.

SARA. Will you go to prison?

TURING. Possibly.

SARA. *(Gazes at him; she cannot prevent a surge of rage.)*
How could you bear to touch a man like that? How could
you do such a thing? *(No response; SARA's anger subsides.)*
How did the police find out? Did they catch you? Did
they find you with this boy?

TURING. I told them. *(TURING gives her a hopeless
shrug.)*

SARA. Oh, Alan.

TURING. I'm sorry. *(Pause; SARA stands looking at her
son.)*

SARA. What can I do to help?

TURING. *(amazed by this)* Well — nothing.

SARA. There must be something I can do. Let me,
please. You look so helpless.

TURING. That's how I feel.

SARA. *(Takes him by the hand.)* Do you remember when
you were at Hazelhurst? You must've been about ten or
eleven. We'd all been up to Scotland for the summer
holidays. Do you remember?

TURING. Yes.

SARA. Daddy went trout-fishing. I sketched. We had
picnic teas in the heather. And then we had to go back to
India, and you had to go back to school, back to
Hazelhurst.

TURING. Yes.

SARA. Do you remember?

TURING. Of course I remember.

SARA. We took a taxi to the school and as we drove

away, you tried to run after us. You ran along the drive after the taxi. Your arms were flung wide; your mouth was open; you were saying something, shouting something, but I couldn't hear what it was. There were some shrubs by the school gates; rhododendrons, I think. It was like a great green curtain being pulled across in front of my eyes. The shrubs hid you from my sight. I couldn't see you any more. For a moment I felt quite breathless with panic. I wanted to jump out of the taxi, run back, and hold you in my arms forever. *(Pause. TURING embraces her.)*

TURING.   I had no idea you felt like that. *(They stand for a moment in still silence; then SARA deliberately breaks the mood.)*

SARA.   Do come and look at the guest room. I'm so pleased with it. *(SARA Exits.)*

Scene 4

SCENE: LIGHTING change: February; rainy afternoon.

AT RISE: ROSS Enters, carrying a file of papers; he sits at the table.

Ross.   Mr. Turing. Sit down. Make yourself comfortable. *(TURING sits.)* You have to sign this first. Got a pen?

TURING.   What is it?

Ross. *(reading)* "I, Alan Mathison Turing, have been told by Detective Sergeant Ross that I am not obliged to make any statement and that what I now say may be given in evidence. On that understanding I make the following statement."

Turing. But you didn't say that. You didn't say I wasn't obliged to make a statement.

Ross. Didn't I, sir?

Turing. Where do I sign?

Ross. There, look — underneath what I've written. *(TURING signs.)* That's fine. *(Brief pause; TURING appears to be waiting for instructions.)* Right then, off you go.

Turing. What do you want me to say?

Ross. Just describe how you met Ron Miller and what happened when he came to your house.

Turing. All right. Um — do you want me to give dates and so on?

Ross. If you can.

Turing. Well. Um. On December the 16th, 1951, I met Ron Miller in a pub near the Oxford Road station in Manchester. I invited him to come to my house on the following Friday evening.

(The rat-a-tat-tat of a front door knocker; TURING walks Upstage and opens the door; RON Enters.)

Ron. Sorry I'm late. Bloody buses. I waited damn near half-an-hour.

Turing. *(Closes the door.)* Take your jacket off. I'll get you a drink.

Ron. I bet you thought I wouldn't show up.

TURING. I thought you might've changed your mind.

RON. I said I'd be here, and here I am. *(TURING smiles, but says nothing.)* Glad to see me?

TURING. Of course. Take your jacket off. *(RON does so; he looks around.)*

RON. Nice place. Been here long?

TURING. Just a few months. A year or so.

RON. Very nice. *(a grin)* Supper smells good.

TURING. *(brighter)* Ah well, I've prepared a sumptuous feast: homemade vegetable soup, roast leg of lamb, roast potatoes, carrots and spinach. Apple pie to follow.

RON. All for a bloke you thought wouldn't show up.

TURING. I hoped.

RON. *(Smiles; brief pause)* What about that drink?

TURING. What would you like?

RON. Got a beer?

TURING. *(Shakes his head.)* Wine or Tizer.

RON. *(surprised)* Tizer...?

TURING. Tizer, Tizer, the appetizer. I'm testing it for its electrical conductivity.

RON. Why?

TURING. No reason. *(playfully)* It's what we call pure research.

RON. *(a frown)* What?

TURING. Nothing. A joke. *(grins)* Hungry?

RON. Starving. *(TURING turns to address ROSS.)*

TURING. We had dinner. A bottle of wine. We talked about my work at the university, then I told him about *War and Peace.*

ROSS. About what?

TURING. The book by Tolstoy. Someone had lent it to me. I found it very impressive. *(TURING resumes his scene with RON.)*

RON. I don't like war stories.

TURING. It's not really a war story. It's about two men. One is called Andrei, the other one is Pierre. Andrei is ambitious and very energetic, but he's frightened of his own feelings. The other one, Pierre, is an extraordinary man. He's awkward, ugly and rather shy, but he's full of good-will and love. I like Pierre. He's a marvellous character.

RON. I bet he gets killed.

TURING. *(He shakes his head.)* Andrei gets killed. He gets shot at the Battle of Borodino. It's a good book. You ought to read it.

RON. The battle of what?

TURING. Borodino.

RON. Never heard of it.

TURING. It's a place in Russia. A famous battle.

RON. I wasn't much good at history.

TURING. Now's your chance to learn. I'll help you. *(RON is doubtful.)* Let me get you a copy of the book.

RON. Okay.

TURING. It's very good. Really.

RON. Okay.

TURING. Give it a try. Do read it.

RON. Yeah, okay. *(a grin)* How about another drink?

TURING. Help yourself. Sorry there's no beer. *(Addresses ROSS.)* I've got an old violin at home. Ron thought it was great fun. I played a couple of tunes on it, then Ron had a go, then we talked some more about my work.

RON. How did it all start?

TURING. What?

RON. You being interested in science and things.

TURING. I've always been interested.

RON. Even as a kid?

TURING. Even then. *(Glances at RON; smiles.)* Yes, even then. When I was a child, numbers, were me friends.

RON. *(a frown)* Your what?

TURING. My friends. You know how it is; you know how children have their own secret, make-believe friends; friends who can always be trusted: dolls or teddy bears or some old piece of blanket they've kept and treasured since they were babies. My friends were numbers. They were so wonderfully reliable; they never broke their own rules. And then, when I was about nine or ten, somebody gave me a book for Christmas: *Natural Wonders Every Child Should Know.* I thought it was the most exciting book I'd ever read. It was, I suppose, looking back, a sort of gentle introduction to the facts of life; there was a lot about chickens and eggs, I remember. But what the writer of that book managed to convey was the idea that life — all life — is really a huge, all-embracing enterprise of science. There was no nonsense about God, or divine creation. It was all science: chemicals, plants, animals, humans. "The body is a machine," he said. How exciting it was to read that! What an audacious, challenging — rather naughty — idea that was. He made life seem like a thrilling experiment. And I longed to take part in it. *(Pause; looks at RON.)* Come here. Come and sit beside me. *(RON hesitates.)*

Ross. And that's when the first offense occured?

Ron. Yes.

Ross. Tell me what happened.

Ron. After supper he told me about his work on the electronic brain. Then he started talking about some books he'd read. Then he asked me to sit next to him on the couch. And then he undid my trousers.

Turing. *(soliloquy)* "Dear Mrs. Morcom, I want to say how sorry I am about Christopher. I should be extremely grateful if you could find me sometime a little snap-shot of him. I shall miss his face so, and the way he used to smile at me sideways."

Ron. We listened to the wireless a bit and he played "Cockles and Mussels" on his violin. I had a go on it. We went to bed about 11 o'clock. He put a towel on the bed sheet.

Turing. *(soliloquy)* In *War and Peace* there's a passage where Pierre meditates on his sense of shame. "I must endure ... what?" he asks. "The disgrace of my name and to my honor? Oh, that's all rubbish!" he cries. "Who is right, who is wrong? No one! While you are alive — live!"

Ron. About 9:00 a.m. Mr. Turing got up and got dressed. He left his jacket on the arm of a chair and I knocked off eight pounds out of it. We went into the parlor again. He leaned over me, put his head on my shoulder, and pulled my hand between his legs. I wanked him again, but he never touched me.

Turing. *(soliloquy)* One thing is certain: a machine that is to imitate the brain must appear to behave as if it has free will. What does that mean?

RON. *(reading his statement)* I didn't do this for my own benefit sexually, but I had heard that you could get paid for it. I will never do it again if I am given a chance. I know that it's wrong.

Ross. Okay, Miller, wait outside. *(RON Exits.)*

TURING. *(soliloquy)*. Tolstoy said that free will is merely an expression denoting what we do not know about the laws of human life. Perhaps it's an illusion. But without that illusion, life would be meaningless. *(ROSS gathers together his papers and puts them into the file; TURING remains motionless; ROSS looks at him.)*

Ross. What on earth made you do it?

TURING. Do what?

Ross. Call the police. Talk about asking for trouble.

TURING. What else could I do?

Ross. Sit still and keep quiet.

TURING. But I'd been robbed.

Ross. Not exactly the crime of the century, was it? *(no response)* All that baloney about a brush salesman ... ! I've never heard such rubbish in all my life. You must think I'm a real prick.

TURING. I didn't want to involve Ron. I had to say something, and I didn't want to involve Ron.

Ross. We'd have found out sooner or later.

TURING. Not necessarily.

Ross. Of course we would. Questions get asked. Answers lead to more questions. "Why is a middle-aged, unmarried professor spending the weekend with a bit of rough from the Oxford Road?" Doesn't need a genius to work that one out.

TURING. *(suddenly angry)* Look, — I'd been robbed. I

knew George had robbed me. Why the hell should he get away with it? If I had said nothing, it'd be like giving in to blackmail, and I refuse to do that!

Ross. Okay, fine, that's your decision. But you must've known what would happen.

Turing. No, that never occurred to me.

Ross. *(eyebrows raised)* Didn't it, sir?

Turing. Not then. Not at the time. I didn't know you'd treat me like a criminal.

Ross. Not much choice, was there? When a man says he's committed a crime, I can't just ignore it.

Turing. Going to bed with Ron is not a crime.

Ross. It's against the law.

Turing. It's not as simple as that.

Ross. In your opinion.

Turing. Is your opinion any better?

Ross. Look, I don't care what you and young Ron get up to. But if it's against the law, I have to do something about it, okay?

Turing. Doesn't that worry you?

Ross. Why should it?

Turing. Because the law makes everything black, white — right, wrong. Life is more complicated than that.

Ross. You mean sex.

Turing. *(irritation)* No, not just sex!

Ross. What, then?

Turing. All sorts of things. Mathematics. Even in mathematics there's no infallible rule for proving what is right and what is wrong. Each problem — each decision — requires fresh ideas, fresh thought. And if that's the case in mathematics — the most reliable body of knowledge that mankind has created — surely it might also apply in other, less certain, areas. *(RON hesitates, thinking, before he replies.)*

Ross. Decisions have to made; and if we can't decide what's right and what's wrong, then we've got to get someone — or something — to decide for us. All we've got is the law — and, in the present circumstances, that means me. *(Picks up the file of papers.)* Nothing personal, Mr. Turing. I understand how you must feel.

Turing. No you don't.

Ross. You're right — I don't.

Turing. How can you?

Ross. I can't. *(Goes to Exit.)* You'll receive official notification of the court proceedings. And keep it simple, sir; all that stuff about mathematics won't go down too well with local magistrates. *(ROSS Exits.)*

Scene 5

SCENE: LIGHTING change: Midday sun.

AT RISE: PAT Enters, carrying picnic food on a tray. TURING spreads a raincoat on the ground.

Turing. What did you get?

Pat. Spam sandwiches, fruit cake and lemonade.

Turing. Delicious.

Pat. There wasn't much of a choice, I'm afraid.

TURING. I'm sorry. I should've taken you to a restaurant.

PAT. *(smiles)* This is fun. *(They start to eat.)* It's good to see you, Prof.

TURING. It's good to see you.

PAT. Thank you for writing to me.

TURING. I wanted you to know what had happened. And I wanted you to hear it from me, not — well, second-hand.

PAT. Thank you.

TURING. It was in the News of the World, Northern Edition. One of the headlines said, "Accused had Powerful Brain." Could've been worse, I suppose — though that use of the past tense rather worried me. *(PAT smiles. They eat in silence for a moment.)*

PAT. I've thought about you a lot. It must've been awful.

TURING. Actually, not as bad as I feared. They put me in the cells during the trial. Being behind bars was by no means disagreeable. There was a wonderful absense of responsibility, rather like being back at school. *(referring to the sandwich)* Is that all right?

PAT. Fine. Did you think they'd send you to prison?

TURING. No, not really; I was a first offender, after all. First offender! — there's a laugh! No, I thought they'd most probably put me on probation. *(brief pause)* They're giving me drugs.

PAT. Who are?

TURING. They're giving me oestrogen: female sex hormones. It's supposed to kill male sexual interest. It's only for a year — after that, everything returns to normal. We hope.

PAT. *(shocked)* That's dreadful. Couldn't you refuse?

TURING. No, I'm obliged to do it. They put me on probation providing I agreed to the drug treatment. *(brief pause)* I'm growing breasts.

PAT. Oh, Alan.

TURING. Nobody seems to know whether or not they'll disappear when I stop taking the drugs. We'll just have to wait and see.

PAT. God, how dreadful.

TURING. The embarrassment factor is high. I keep wondering if I'll have to wear a bra. *(He smiles; PAT remains silent.)* It was awful going back to work after the trial. I didn't know how my colleagues would behave. I feared the worst. I was right. Oh, the weird ideas people have about homosexuals. *(brief pause)* There was a predictable reaction from my brother.

PAT. Brother John.

TURING. Brother John. Disgusted, repelled, incredulous, et cetera. He said I'd been a silly ass to go to the police. He was right.

PAT. What about your mother?

TURING. Yes, I dreaded telling her. I absolutely dreaded it. As it happens, she was wonderful. Quite remarkable. It seems to have drawn us closer together.

PAT. I'm glad.

TURING. So am I. *(pause)*

PAT. What happened to the boy? The boy who, um...

TURING. Conditionally discharged. He's working in London, I think. I never see him. *(brief pause)* Are you married?

PAT. Yes.

TURING. No job?

PAT. Just a housewife.

TURING. Are you happy?

PAT. Yes. Well, I suppose so. I don't think about it very much.

TURING. That means you are.

PAT. Does it?

TURING. You only think about being happy when you're not. Any children?

PAT. Two. Two boys.

TURING. I should have liked to have had children. Is that a very sentimental thing to say?

PAT. Not in the least.

TURING. It sounds sentimental, coming from an old poof like me.

PAT. Don't say such things.

TURING. It was supposed to be a joke.

PAT. *(Looks at him: concerned, tender.)* I hope you're not too unhappy.

TURING. I'm not unhappy at all. I enjoy my work; I have some good friends. I had a very jolly holiday. Norway.

PAT. *(surprised)* Norway...?

TURING. No legal problems in Norway. I was told there were places where they held dances for men only. Not true, alas. But I did meet a charming young man called Kjell. He wrote to me last week, as a matter of fact; wants to spend a few days *chez moi*. I obviously made a good impression.

PAT. *(Smiles; brief pause.)* What sort of work are you doing?

TURING. I'm at Manchester University.

PAT. Yes, I know.

TURING. *(animated)* We've built a digital computer. You remember all my theorizing about a universal machine? Well, we've done it, we've made one — and it's all thanks to the war, really. It's all thanks to the work we did at Bletchley.

PAT. Why?

TURING. Electronics.

PAT. How?

TURING. Until we did it at Bletchley, nobody had thought of using electronics to carry out logical operations. And that's just what I needed — because a computer would have to carry out hundreds of thousands of logical operations every second. Electronics gave us the necessary speed — which left us with problem number two: memory. A computer must keep a huge store of instructions and information in its memory — how was this to be achieved? At first, we created a memory by using an acoustic delay line.

PAT. Using sound waves?

TURING. *(a nod)* It takes a thousandth of a second for a sound wave to travel along a few feet of pipe; so for that period the pipe could be said to be storing the sound wave.

PAT. The radar people used that idea during the war.

TURING. Yes — we pinched it. We used a delay line to store the pulses of an electronic computer. But now, at Manchester, we're using little television screens — which means you can actually see the numbers and instructions stored in the machine. You can see them on the monitor tube: little bright dots.

PAT. How exciting. It must be very exciting.

TURING. Well, it would be if the organization wasn't so rigid. Everything is so compartmentalized. You're either a mathematician or an engineer; you can't be both.

PAT. Unlike Bletchley.

TURING. Totally unlike Bletchley, more's the pity. But at least I'm able to use the computer for my own work. I've become increasingly interested in morphogenesis.

PAT. *(surprised)* Embryology?

TURING. How do living things take shape? How do things know how to grow? I've got an idea what might explain that — and I'm using the computer to simulate the growth patterns of plants and animals. Like the Fibonacci patterns in a fir cone. Do you remember me telling you about that?

PAT. Yes.

TURING. One summer afternoon, when you thought you were in love with me.

PAT. I went to church with your mother and cried all through the sermon.

TURING. *(Looks at her; he reaches out, gently touching her hand.)* You haven't changed at all, do you know that?

PAT. *(smiles)* It's nice of you to say so.

TURING. It's true. *(brief pause)* It seems an awfully long time since we were at Bletchley.

PAT. Doesn't it?

TURING. A lifetime. *(brief pause)* I never found that silver.

PAT. What silver?

TURING. Those silver ingots I buried.

PAT. *(smiles)* Oh yes.

TURING. I searched high and low. Never found them.

PAT. I wonder if your tea mug is still chained to the radiator.

TURING. *(smiles)* Yes, I got told off about that.

PAT. Who by?

TURING. Dilwyn Knox.

PAT. Poor Mr. Knox. *(a sigh)* I went to see him when he was ill — near the end.

TURING. That was good of you.

PAT. I was fond of him. He was so ill they were saying prayers for him in church. Mr. Knox was furious about it. "Christianity is a two-thousand-year-old swindle," he said; "It makes you fear when there is nothing to fear, and hope when there is nothing to hope for."

TURING. *(smiles)* He was a remarkable man.

PAT. He was. *(brief pause)* I suppose you knew he was a homosexual?

TURING. *(incredulous)* What?

PAT. Homosexually inclined, anyway. He's supposed to have had some sort of a romance with Maynard Keynes.

TURING. Knox...?

PAT. When he was young.

TURING. Are you sure?

PAT. An uncle of mine was at school with him.

TURING. Good God.

PAT. Lytton Strachey, too — but that was a Cambridge, not Eton.

TURING. *(amazed)* He was Lytton Strachey's lover...?!

PAT. Apparently. I thought you knew.

TURING. I hadn't the faintest idea.

PAT. Well, I don't think anybody paid much attention to it. Everything's so very different when you're at school or at university.

TURING. Good God Almighty.

PAT. And it was all a thing of the past; he was devoted to his wife.

TURING. Yes, he told me. *(glancing at PAT)* That's the thing to do, of course: have your fling when you're young and conform later. I should've married you. All this would never have happened. I should've played the game and stuck to the rules.

PAT. Why didn't you?

TURING. I couldn't.

PAT. *(gently mocking him)* Silly ass.

TURING. *(smiles)* Yes. *(Brief pause. PAT stands up.)*

PAT. Would you like an ice cream?

TURING. I'll get it.

PAT. My treat. Cone or wafer?

TURING. Er — wafer. No — cone. *(PAT Exits.)*

Scene 6

SCENE: LIGHTING change: Late afternoon, darkening skies.

AT RISE: JOHN SMITH Enters: The authoritative man last seen in Act I, Scene 4.

SMITH. Mr. Turing? I'm sorry to keep you waiting. Everything's at sixes and sevens here today. *(He shakes hands with TURING.)* My secretary's gone down with 'flu, and the temporary girl doesn't seem to know what she's doing. *(taking TURING'S coat)* May I? *(Gestures to chair.)* Please sit there. It's good of you to come along at such short notice. Thank you very much. *(TURING sits.)*

TURING. Your letter was rather vague.

SMITH. Was it?

TURING. Official, but rather vague.

SMITH. Well, it's just one of those things that are done better by a meeting than by telephone. Basically it's a question of keeping in touch.

TURING. What do you mean?

SMITH. You're a brilliant man, Mr. Turing — unique in many ways — and there's no point in trying to deny it.

TURING. I wasn't going to.

SMITH. This country has always tended to take its brilliant men for granted. That's a mistake. A serious mistake. We can't afford to make mistakes like that.

TURING. Who are you? I've no idea who you are.

SMITH. Sorry, sorry, sorry. My name is Smith, John Smith. *(smiles)* Nobody believes it. I have a dreadful time with hotel clerks. Anyway, the point is this: it would be foolish to pretend that your homosexuality hasn't created certain problems, certain anxieties.

TURING. *(bristling)* For whom?

SMITH. *(ignoring this)* But providing we can discuss the situation reasonably, I feel sure that these anxieties can be reduced to a minimum.

TURING. What anxieties?

SMITH. As I say, it's just a question of keeping in touch.

TURING. You're talking about security problems.

SMITH. I am. Of course, I know you haven't been involved with intelligence work since your, uh, little difficulty with the law; nevertheless, the knowledge remains, does it not?

TURING. *(angry)* You don't trust me.

SMITH. We have to be careful. Increasingly careful. An unguarded word could so easily fall into the wrong ears. And it's not just us. The Americans are getting jumpy, and we have to pay atttention to what they say, we have to. After all, they've given you accesss to some very sensitive information — the speech encipherment materials, for instance. And thanks to Senator McCarthy, they regard everyone as a potential security risk. *(TURING looks at him; says nothing.)* There is a general feeling of unease.

TURING. About me?

SMITH. Of course we know that you are a man of the greatest integrity. Your essential loyalty has never been questioned.

TURING. *(voicing the unspoken word)* But.

SMITH. All possibilities have to be considered.

TURING. Such as?

SMITH. Can you, in all honesty, say that you would never — never, under any circumstances — reveal something of the nature of your work to a sexual partner? *(TURING opens his mouth to make an immediate response, but then hesitates for a moment.)*

TURING. No, of course not.

SMITH. No, you would — or no, you wouldn't?

TURING. No, I can't say — in all honesty — that such a circumstance would never arise. Neither can you. Who could?

SMITH. *(smoothly avoiding a direct response)* That being the case, one's attention is drawn to the choice of partner. *(briefest pause)* It seems that you have an unusually wide range of acquaintances.

TURING. You mean it would be all right if I went to bed with other mathematicians? Preferably from one of the older universities. Preferably with what the Americans call Security Clearance.

SMITH. *(dryly)* I'm sure that would make us a lot happier. *(a glance at TURING)* Sorry, that was rather glib. But you must realize that your work for the intelligence service means that you are simply not free to behave as you might choose. You have been given extremely unusual access to secret information. This carries with it a heavy and sometimes irksome responsibility.

TURING. *(Angered by SMITH'S patronizing tone.)* I am aware of that.

SMITH. *(chastened)* Yes, I'm sure you are. *(brief pause)* It may seem like interference; in fact, we're trying to be helpful.

TURING. Oh? How?

SMITH. By preventing any further errors of judgement.

TURING. Meaning what exactly?

SMITH. This young Norwegian — Kjell. *(TURING is amazed.)* I think it would be unwise for him to visit you here.

TURING. How do you know about Kjell?

SMITH. Somebody told me.

TURING. Who?

SMITH. I forget. *(TURING is sceptical.)* Truly.

TURING. Am I being watched?

SMITH. You're a valuable man. You have valuable information stored away inside that — what did you call it? — inside that bowl of cold porridge. *(small smile)* I have a nephew at Sherborne. He was most impressed by your lecture. *(brief pause)* We have to make sure that this knowledge is properly protected. *(TURING is silent, apparently considering the situation; SMITH looks at him.)* I can guess what's going through your mind.

TURING. Can you?

SMITH. You're feeling outraged; outraged and resentful.

TURING. As a matter of fact, I was thinking about the Duke of Windsor. I was appalled by the way he was bounced into exile. Most particularly, I was appalled by the hypocrisy of the Establishment: Mrs. Simpson was okay as his mistress, but as his wife — never! I felt it was shameful of the State to interfere with a man's private life; and I was convinced that the government wanted to get rid of him and used Mrs. Simpson merely as as excuse. *(brief pause)* But then later, I heard that he'd been extremely lax about state documents, leaving them about and letting Mrs. Simpson and her friends see them. I changed my mind about the abdication. A man who does that shouldn't be King. *(pause)* When you say "keeping in touch," what precisely do you mean?

SMITH. We'd like to be told about any change of residence,

any change in your working life, any trips abroad, that sort of thing. Are you planning to go abroad this year?

TURING. Yes, I'm going to Greece.

SMITH. When?

TURING. May.

SMITH. Whereabouts in Greece?

TURING. Corfu.

SMITH. Oh, it's very nice there, you'll like it a lot; and May is the perfect time to go. *(TURING and SMITH stand facing each other; pause.)*

TURING. I want you to know that I have no regrets about my involvement with the intelligence service. The work I did at Bletchley was very important to me.

SMITH. Yes, I'm sure.

TURING. Important in a way you probably cannot understand. It took much more than mathematics and electronic ingenuity to break the U-boat Enigma. I needed determination, tenacity — moral fiber, if you like. That's what made it so deeply satisfying. Everything came together there. All the strands of my life came together. My work as a mathematician. My interest in ciphers. My ability to solve practical problems. My love of my country. You trusted me then. Why not now? *(SMITH Exits.)*

Scene 7

SCENE: LIGHTING change: Bars of sunshine through shuttered windows.

AT RISE: NIKOS, a Greek boy of about 20, lies face down on a divan; asleep; naked, apart from a towel wrapped around his waist. An abandoned sheet lies on the floor; nearby, on a table, is a large, old-fashioned radio.

TURING goes to the divan and looks down at NIKOS.

TURING. Are you really asleep or are you just pretending? *(No response; he smiles.)* Nikos from Ipsos. Never before have I been to bed with someone I couldn't talk to. The Greek phrasebook doesn't cover these circumstances, alas. *(Looks at watch.)* Half past five. That means it's —what? — half past three at home. They'll soon be having tea and buns in the laboratory. *(Wanders across the room: sees the radio.)* My God, look at the wireless! A real museum piece. *(Switches on the radio; nothing happens.)* Doesn't work. Never mind. Mustn't expect too much in this life. *(Sleepily, NIKOS looks at TURING and the radio.)*

    NIKOS. Den doulevi. [It doesn't work.]
    TURING. This thing doesn't work.
    NIKOS. Den doulevi.
    TURING. Your wireless doesn't work.
    NIKOS. Ine spasmino. [It's broken.]

97

TURING. Is that what you're telling me? Are you saying it doesn't work?

NIKOS. Ine spasmino.

TURING. I'll mend it for you, shall I? *(Tries to mime mending the radio.)* Would you like me to do that? Shall I try?

NIKOS. *(Stares at him.)* Den katalaveno. [I don't understand.]

TURING. Perhaps I can mend it. I used to be rather good at that sort of thing. *(More mime.)* Me — mend — wireless — okay?

NIKOS. Borite na to diorthosete? [You can mend it?]

TURING. I'll need a screwdriver. *(More mime.)* Do you have a screwdriver?

NIKOS. *(Understands; a beaming smile.)* Hriazeste ena katsavidi! Tha sas vro ena ... [You need a screwdriver! I'll find you one...] *(NIKOS Exits; TURING examines the radio.)*

TURING. Let's have a look at it. I've always taken a particular pride in my practical skills. What's the point of being a theorist if you can't put your theories into practice? Ah, yes — I see what's wrong ... *(NIKOS Enters, holding a screwdriver.)*

NIKOS. Katsavidi. [Screwdriver.]

TURING. Oh good, you've found one.

NIKOS. Katsavidi.

TURING. *(taking the screwdriver)* Thank you.

NIKOS. *(emphatically)* Katsavidi.

TURING. Oh — that's the word, is it?

NIKOS. Katsavidi!

TURING. Katsavidi.

NIKOS. *(grinning)* Ne — katsavidi!

TURING. Katsavidi. Well, that's wonderful, thank you very much. If I ever need to buy a screwdriver in Greece, I'll know just what to ask for. *(He smiles at NIKOS.)* You're a very good listener. Nikos from Ipsos. You ought to have been a Jungian analyst. *(As he talks, he mends the radio.)* I went to an analyst for a time. About a couple of years ago. There'd been some trouble with the police. I was prosecuted for an offense the British quaintly call Gross Indecency. It was a very disturbing and unpleasant experience. That's why I went to the analyst. I told him everything. Almost. Even my dreams. He'd just sit there and listen. Rather like you, Nikos from Ipsos. He'd sit there and listen and listen and listen. The idea, you see, was to integrate thinking and feeling. That's the basis of Jungian analysis: the integration of thinking and feeling. A tall order, in my case. *(He gestures to the radio.)* Right. Good. There you are, then. That should work now.

NIKOS. Toftiaxes? [You fixed it?]

TURING. Switch it on.

NIKOS. Endaxi? Etimo? [All right? Ready?]

TURING. Switch it on.

(NIKOS steps forward cautiously; he switches on the radio; a loud burst of Greek dance music; NIKOS shouts with delight and embraces TURING.)

NIKOS. To diorthosete! To kabate na doulevi! [You've mended it! You've made it work!]

TURING. Thank you, thank you — that's enough. *(TURING disentagles himself from NIKOS'S embrace and switches off the radio.)*

NIKOS. Iste poli exypnos — poli exypnos anthropos. Afto to radio den doulepse yia pollous mines. To pira sena filo pou xeri apo radia, ke ipe ine para poli palio, ke pote den the xanadoulepsi. Ma ine kalo radio — to xero — re yiafto to filaxa. Den borousa ne to petaxo. Ka tora to kanate na doulevi. Iste poli exypnos anthropos! [You are very clever — a very clever man. That radio hasn't worked for many months. I took it to a friend who knows about radios, and he said it was too old, it would never work again. But it's a good radio — I know that — and so I kept it. I couldn't bear to throw it away. And now you have fixed it. You have made it work. You are a very clever man!]

TURING. Well, I've no idea what that was all about — but I'm glad you're so pleased.

NIKOS. Iste poli exypnos anthropos! [You are a very clever man!] *(NIKOS kisses TURING, who is both touched and embarrassed.)*

TURING. Thank you, Nikos dear. Thank you. *(smiles.)* It's a good feeling, isn't it? Solving a problem, finding the answer. Making it work. A good feeling. It's all like that wireless, really, it's all a question of making the right connections. *(A brief pause; an idea slips into his mind.)* Shall I tell you a secret? Top secret. I couldn't even tell my analyst about this. But since you won't understand a single word, it doesn't really matter. It all took place at the beginning of the war in a country house called Bletchley Park. The Germans had built a machine called the Enigma. It was very cunning. It made codes — and nobody knew how to break the codes it made. That was the problem we had to

solve. If we didn't, if we couldn't we'd lose the war — it
was as simple as that. But where to begin? Well, first there
was guess-work. The codebreaking process always began
with a guess. You had to guess what the first few letters of
the message might mean. This wasn't as difficult as it
sounds because military messages invariable start with a
stereotyped phrase: The date, the time, the name and
rank of the sender, that sort of thing. Then we discovered
that it was possible to use the phrase we guessed to form a
chain of implications, of logical deductions, for each of
the rotor positions. If this chain of implications led you
to a contradiction — which was usually the case — that
meant you were wrong, and you'd have to move onto the
next position. And so on and so on. An impossibly
lengthy and laborious process: time was against us. We
didn't know what to do. And then, one afternoon, I
remembered a conversation I'd had with Wittgenstein:
we were arguing about the fact that a contradiction
implied any proposition. And I saw — immediately —
how I could use this elementary theorem in mathematical logic to build a machine that would have the
necessary speed: a machine with electrical relays and
logical circuits which would sense contradictions and
recognize consistencies; a machine of cribs, closed loops,
and perfect synchrony; a machine for discerning a pattern in the patternless. If your guess was wrong, then the
electricity would flow though all the related hypotheses
and knock them out in a flash — like the chain reaction in
an atomic bomb. If your guess was correct, everything
would be consistent — and the electrical current would
stop at the correct combination. Our machine could

examine thousands of millions of permutations at amazing speed — and, with any luck, would give us the "way in." More than that: all the connections had been made. There was the pure beauty of the logical pattern. The human element. The deeply satisfying relationship between the theoretical and the practical. What a moment that was. Quite, quite extraordinary. *(pause)* Oh, Christopher ... If only you could've been there. Never again. Never again a moment like that. *(pause)* In the long run, it's not breaking the code that matters — it's where you go from there. That's the real problem.

Scene 8

SCENE: LIGHTING change: Grey afternoon in Manchester.

AT RISE: The telephone rings. ROSS hurries to the telephone; he is carrying a cardboard box; he puts the box on the table and grabs the telephone receiver.

Ross. Hello, Ross ... Okay, fine. *(Hangs up and goes to the door.)* Come in, Mrs. Turing.

(SARA Enters.)

Ross. Do sit down. Can I get you a cup of tea or something? A cup of coffee? *(SARA sits.)*
Sara. No, thank you.

Ross. Right, um *(indicating the cardboard box)* — these are your son's personal belongings. As you know, a few odds and ends had to be examined before the coroner could complete his report. Here's a list; you'd better make sure everything's there.

SARA. Do I have to?

Ross. Not if it upsets you.

SARA. I think I'd rather not. *(ROSS takes an envelope from his jacket pocket and gives it to SARA.)*

Ross. I kept this separately. It's his medal, his O.B.E. I was afraid it might get lost.

SARA. *(Puts it into her handbag.)* Thank you.

Ross. *(Gives her a document.)* If you'll just sign here, please. *(SARA signs.)* Good, thank you. *(Takes the document.)* I didn't know he'd got the O.B.E. He never told me. What was it for?

SARA. The work he did during the war. Whatever that was. *(sighs)* There are so many things I know nothing about; so many things I don't understand.

Ross. Yes, it's a sad business. I'm very sorry.

SARA. Of course, it was all a dreadful mistake.

Ross. In what way?

SARA. The coroner's verdict.

Ross. *(noncommittal)* Ah, well...

SARA. To say that Alan took his own life is quite ridiculous. Everyone knew he did experiments at home and he never washed his hands, never. It was obviously a tragic accident.

Ross. I can't really offer an opinion, Mrs. Turing.

SARA. You met him. Do you think he was the sort of man to commit suicide?

Ross. It's two or three years since I've seen him, and you never know what people might do in extreme circumstances.

Sara. Let me tell you something about my son. His first day at Sherborne was also the first day of the General Strike. He bicycled all the way from Southampton to Sherborne — sixty miles! — so he would be sure of getting to school on time. It was reported in the local newspaper. A boy who could do that would never take his own life. He had everything to live for. Everything.

Scene 9

AT RISE: TURING is sitting Downstage.

Turing. What is needed is the ability to take ideas seriously and to follow them through to their logical if upsetting conclusion. Thus. Can the mind exist without the body? Can mental processes take place in something other than a living brain? How are we to answer that question satisfactorily? Is it possible to do so? Or is it simply an eternal *Entscheidungsproblem?* Forever undecidable ... *(Pause, then almost vivaciously.)* Being a practical man as well as a theorist, I tend to look for practical solutions; in this case namely, viz., to dispose of the body and to release what is left. A mind. Or a nothing. *(He takes out an apple and a small tin.)* Here I have an ordinary apple:

red and ripe and English. And here — a tin containing potassium cyanide. *(The ghost of a smile.)* Nothing could be easier, could it? *(Dips the apple into the potassium cyanide and raises the fruit to his lips.)* Dip the apple in the brew, let the sleeping death seep through.

CURTAIN

COSTUME PLOT

DILLWYN KNOX
Green tweed 3-piece suit (doesn't wear vest)
Green plaid wool shirt
Red-on-cream tattersall wool shirt
Suspenders
Green wide-rib socks
Brown shoes
Cufflinks
Gold-rimmed spectacles & case
Pipe
2 handkerchiefs
Wedding ring
Wristwatch

RON MILLER
Brown pants
Suspenders
Fishnet undershirt
Red sweater
Tan windbreaker
Red-patterned socks
Dark grey suede shoes

MICK ROSS
Grey hat
Raincoat
Brown-plaid scarf

3-piece Glen plaid suit
White shirt
Dark tie w/dots
Black shoes
Black socks
Suspenders
Wedding ring
Wristwatch

NIKOS
Tan undershirt
Tan trousers
Suspenders
Espadrilles (for backstage and curtain calls)

CHRISTOPHER MORCOM
Grey 2-piece wool suit
Black raincoat
Blue shirt
Blue/black striped tie
Blue/black striped cap
Wool gloves (pinned in coat pocket)
Suspenders
Pencils (in suit breast pocket)
Black shoes
Grey wool socks
Blue wool sleeveless sweater

SMITH
THRUOUT:
White shirt

Wristwatch
Black shoes
Black socks
Gold/onyx pinkie ring

ACT I:
3-piece striped suit
Dark striped tie
Black overcoat
Black derby hat
Suspenders
White handkerchief (in suit breast pocket)
Black leather gloves
Black umbrella

ACT II:
Black coat and vest
Grey striped trousers
Suspenders
Black tie
Watchchain

SARA TURING
ACT I, SC. 2:
Cream wool/chiffon dress
Cream linen jacket
Cream straw hat
Half slip
Stockings w/seams
Cream linen shoes
Drop pearl earrings

Long single strand pearl necklace
Marchisite brooch
Wedding band & pearl ring

ACT I, SC. 7:
Cream plaid wool dress w/self belt
Brown shoes
3-strand pearl necklace
Gold & pearl earrings
Wristwatch
Pearl ring

ACT II, SC. 3:
Green wool dress w/belt
Dark navy shoes
3-strand pearl necklace
Mustard cardigan sweater (man's style)
Wedding band, only

ACT II, SC. 8:
Print silk dress w/belt
Navy print coat
Navy straw hat
Navy purse
Navy gloves
Black shoes
3-strand pearl necklace

THRUOUT:
Seamed pantyhose
Wig

PAT GREEN
ACT I. SC. 5:
Cream silk blouse, long-sleeved
Brown wool skirt w/leather belt
Grey lab coat
Brown Oxford shoes
Wristwatch

ACT I, SC. 7: (Note: This is a quick change.)
Beige print silk dress w/self belt
Bone sling-back shoes w/bows
Pearl necklace
Pearl starburst earrings
Gold bracelet
Wristwatch

ACT II:
Cream silk blouse, short-sleeved
2-piece brown tweed suit w/pleated skirt
Brown velvet hat
Brown leather purse
Brown gloves
2-tone brown pumps
Amber beaded earrings
Wedding band

THRUOUT:
Seamed pantyhose
Wig (style change for II)

ALAN TURING
ACT I:
Underdress:
　Purple running T-shirt
　White shorts
　Thick navy-blue wool socks
Striped shirt
Tweed trousers w/suspenders
Maroon sleeveless sweater
Brown lace-up shoes
Dirty white handkerchief
Striped silk scarf
Brown wool checked dressing gown
Tweed jacket w/elbow patches
Green wool tie
Beige gabardine raincoat
Blue striped school cap

ACT II:
Striped shirt
Tweed trousers *w/out* suspenders
Brown lace-up shoes
Short beige socks
Leather belt
Dirty white handkerchief
Leather belt
Tweed jacket w/elbow patches
Blue/red striped tie
Brown/beige sleeveless sweater
Brown wool checked dressing gown
Beige gabardine raincoat

PROP LIST

Buff folder and papers
Pens and cartridges
Pencils
Leather briefcase
Double pocket file
Folders
1 pipe
2 pairs of spectacles
Brown wooden tray
Silver metal tray
2 glass jugs
6 tumblers
2 pint beer mugs
2 small ridged glasses
2 plain glasses
Bag of corks
2 lemonade bottles
2 glass sugar bowls
4 wine glasses
Paper straws
2 fir cones
1 posy bowl
1 towel
4 white china plates
1 bunch artificial flowers
1 sponge
Green paper file

Grey paper file
2 cardboard boxes
1 metal box
1 cane
2 screwdrivers
1 small tin w/lid
1 radio
1 wooden box
Wine bottle
4 telephones
3 telephone hand sets
2 suitcases
Peanut packet and paper
2 exercise books
1 leather wallet
9 prop £1 notes and 6 spares
Leather file
2 whiskey bottles
Tray cloths
Wooden shelf for back of sofa
Doorknock
Paper doilies
"Tizer" bottle and labels

FURNITURE:
4 metal chairs and 2 spares
Trolley
2 director's chairs and 4 spares
Large green wooden table
2 stools
Round metal cafe table

Armchair
Footstool
Filing cabinet
Sofa w/4 pillows
Square metal table

2 Equity cots
7 refrigerators
1 vacuum cleaner and attachments
Touch-up paint
1 two-drawer filing cabinet

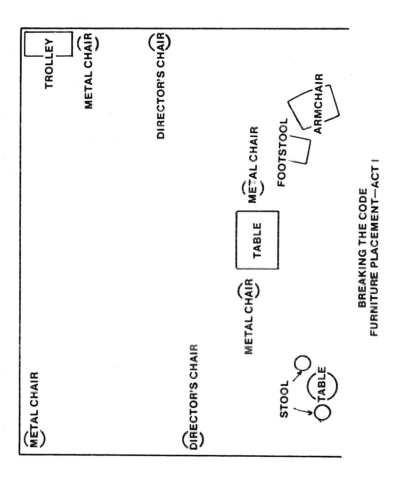

BREAKING THE CODE
FURNITURE PLACEMENT—ACT I

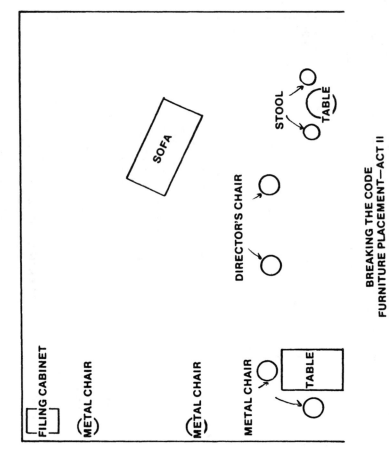

BREAKING THE CODE
FURNITURE PLACEMENT—ACT II

HUGH WHITEMORE

. . . began his career in British television, writing many plays, dramatizations and serials, and twice winning Writer's Guild Awards. He has also written for American television, most notably CONCEALED ENEMIES, a four-hour film about the Alger Hiss case which won the 1984 Emmy for best mini-series. His credits include scripts for several British and American movies. His most recent screenplay is for Mel Brooks' production of 84 CHARING CROSS ROAD (starring Anne Bancroft and Anthony Hopkins, directed by David Jones), which was selected for the 1987 Royal Film Performance. His stage plays are *STEVIE (1977, starring Glenda Jackson) and *PACK OF LIES (1983 starring Judi Dench; Broadway 1984, starring Rosemary Harris). Both plays were directed by Clifford Williams. The film version of STEVIE enjoyed a great success in New York in 1982, and PACK OF LIES was screened in 1987 as a Hallmark Hall of Fame presentation, starring Ellen Burstyn, Teri Garr and Alan Bates. Mr. Whitemore's new play, THE BEST OF FRIENDS, also had a successful run in London, starring Sir John Gielgud, Rosemary Harris and Ray McAnally.

THE SCENE
Theresa Rebeck

Little Theatre / Drama / 2m, 2f / Interior Unit Set
A young social climber leads an actor into an extra-marital affair, from which he then creates a full-on downward spiral into alcoholism and bummery. His wife runs off with his best friend, his girlfriend leaves, and he's left with… nothing.

"Ms. Rebeck's dark-hued morality tale contains enough fresh insights into the cultural landscape to freshen what is essentially a classic boy-meets-bad-girl story."
- New York Times

"Rebeck's wickedly scathing observations about the sort of self-obsessed New Yorkers who pursue their own interests at the cost of their morality and loyalty."
- New York Post

"The Scene is utterly delightful in its comedic performances, and its slowly unraveling plot is thought-provoking and gut-wrenching."
- Show Business Weekly

THE OFFICE PLAYS
Two full length plays by Adam Bock

THE RECEPTIONIST
Comedy / 2m., 2f. Interior

At the start of a typical day in the Northeast Office, Beverly deals effortlessly with ringing phones and her colleague's romantic troubles. But the appearance of a charming rep from the Central Office disrupts the friendly routine. And as the true nature of the company's business becomes apparent, The Receptionist raises disquieting, provocative questions about the consequences of complicity with evil.

"...Mr. Bock's poisoned Post-it note of a play."
New York Times

"Bock's intense initial focus on the routine goes to the heart of *The Receptionist's* pointed, painfully timely allegory... elliptical, provocative play..."
- Time Out New York

THE THUGS
Comedy / 2m, 6f / Interior

The Obie Award winning dark comedy about work, thunder and the mysterious things that are happening on the 9th floor of a big law firm. When a group of temps try to discover the secrets that lurk in the hidden crevices of their workplace, they realize they would rather believe in gossip and rumors than face dangerous realities.

"Bock starts you off giggling, but leaves you with a chill."
- Time Out New York

"... a delightfully paranoid little nightmare that is both more chillingly realistic and pointedly absurd than anything John Grisham ever dreamed up."
- New York Times

SAMUELFRENCH.COM

CPSIA information can be obtained at www.ICGtesting.com
Printed in the USA
LVOW10s0740230714

395534LV00011B/211/P